I0668920

The Berserker's Bride

by

Laura Strickland

This is a work of fiction. Names, characters, places, and incidents are either the product of the author's imagination or are used fictitiously, and any resemblance to actual persons living or dead, business establishments, events, or locales, is entirely coincidental.

The Berserker's Bride

COPYRIGHT © 2019 by Laura Strickland

All rights reserved. No part of this book may be used or reproduced in any manner whatsoever without written permission of the author or The Wild Rose Press, Inc. except in the case of brief quotations embodied in critical articles or reviews.
Contact Information: info@thewildrosepress.com

Cover Art by *Diana Carlile*

The Wild Rose Press, Inc.
PO Box 708
Adams Basin, NY 14410-0708
Visit us at www.thewildrosepress.com

Publishing History
First Tea Rose Edition, 2019
Print ISBN 978-1-5092-2847-8
Digital ISBN 978-1-5092-2848-5

Published in the United States of America

He turned where he stood to survey her again. He could not seem to get his fill of looking. Ah, by Odin's eye, what a fool he was! Burdening himself with a woman, of all things, even out of pity, only further complicated his life.

He certainly did not need any more complications, though he had to admit his dwelling could use a good sweep and scrub. Would this Eadha be a competent and willing worker? Something about her declared her less than versed in things domestic, with a streak, perhaps, of the wild.

Ja, and that went to the heart of it, what he had sensed about her back in Gunnar's hall that made him speak out as never before.

Perhaps she would prove attractive, once clean and properly clothed. In the light of the hall, her tangled hair had carried a reddish gleam. Her face, with its sharp cheekbones, freckled skin, and that odd mark on the cheek, looked foreign enough to fire the passion of one such as Friti.

He, Tolljur, tended to pour all his passion into the madness when it took him.

What color were her eyes? He had not been able to tell in the hall and could not see them well enough now. Would she ruin them spending her time weeping and moping for her husband back in the islands? Had she the wit to accept her lot, safer here with him than elsewhere around Husavik?

He grimaced. For this very reason had he never taken a slave; he knew too well how it felt to be held captive to a higher power and forced to serve.

Praise for Laura Strickland

Laura Strickland's novella *FORGED BY LOVE* won first place in the short historical category of the International Digital Awards.

~*~

"The world building is phenomenal."
~*Daysie W. at My Book Addiction and More*

~*~

"Laura Strickland creates a world that not only draws you in, but she incorporates it…seamlessly.…the kind of book that keeps you awake well into the wee hours, and sighing with satisfaction when you've finished the very last page."

~*Nicole McCaffrey, author*

~*~

"As I read I became so involved with the story, I found it difficult to put down the book.…Definitely…an author to watch."

~*Dandelion at Long & Short Reviews*

~*~

"Laura Strickland takes us beyond the fairy tale and ballroom and gives the readers a story full of pain and heartbreak, wonderfully balanced with hope and love."

~*Elissa Blabac, InD'tale Magazine*

~*~

"What follows will make you cry, angry, and appreciative of your own life."

~*Lisa O'Connor, Author and Reviewer*

Dedication

To Ken Gillis,
who has a weakness for my stories, and for Vikings

Chapter One

Husavik, Iceland—Summer 907

Chin up, lass. Do not let them see you stumble or fall.

The words echoed in Eadha MacEwan's head, as they had some hundred times since she'd been forced from her home on Harris, in the Western Isles. They'd pounded through her mind during the attack, and when the fearsome Norse warriors captured her and her fellow clanswomen. They'd murmured in a susurration that sounded like the sea when sickness wracked her body during the long voyage, heading she knew not where—north and west was all she could tell. They'd provided a muttered backdrop to the many days' confinement, with the other captives, in the open pen.

She might be accustomed to hearing voices in her head—at least, she might well be accustomed to catching others' thoughts and feelings, a right torment now. But whose words were these, attempting to buoy her up, and bidding her to find courage? Her father's? Nay, for she'd seen him fall beneath a Norseman's blade, and he quite likely lay dead. Did she, rather, hear the voice of aged Neal, who'd taught her the old ways? She could not tell.

A wonder she could hear any voice at all, for the great hall she now entered—the hall of the Norse warriors—roared with sound. She and the other women had been able to hear the beginning of the celebration even from their vile pen. And when the Norse guards came to bring them hence, Eadha's resolve threatened to fail her. What new horror might she go to meet? What would befall her and her companions now?

The atmosphere in the lofty hall—not round, like their dun back home, but long and boasting high, carved rafters—assaulted Eadha's senses. Scores of male voices, uplifted in cries of triumph, echoed deafeningly, and she could feel far too much: the maddened waves of victorious glee emanating from these monsters in whose hands she and her companions had landed, the grief of her exiled sisters. Aye, a celebration this was—but not for her and those with her.

Hold hard, lass. Show them of what Donnacht MacEwan's daughter is made.

Aye, but I am afraid. She did not like admitting it, even to the unidentified voice. Yet she seemed to have little left of strength or dignity. Her knees trembled beneath her, and she wanted to shrink from all the eyes that turned their way, and from the reek of the place, a combination of male sweat and something far sweeter that hinted at heather ale. She whispered a prayer under her breath to the great god Lugh, as she had so many times before—*Sustain me.* Ah, was it Lugh's voice she heard, proof that the shining one had not abandoned her, after all? Then why did she feel so utterly abandoned?

Eadha's fellow captives moved closer to her, tightening the little flock they'd formed, as might hens when encircled by foxes. By all that was holy, Eadha would save them all if she could, even before she might save herself. She'd tried arguing with the brutes who had seized them, tried bargaining and reasoning—for surprisingly they possessed a rudimentary knowledge of her tongue—all to no avail. The other women ranged in age from girlhood to young mothers, many of them still sick from the voyage and barely able to stand. She squeezed her eyes shut in a desperate attempt to shut away the sound, the horror and the danger, and prayed for a miracle.

Lugh, please.

"Eadha, Eadha!" Suddenly, as if in answer to her prayer, she heard herself called by name. Her eyes flew open, and she stiffened when a body pressed in close beside her. What new danger this, where danger loomed on every side? Nay, for this voice and face she knew. A miracle, surely, the first she'd encountered since leaving home.

"Catrin!" she gasped in disbelief, staring into the face of her own clanswoman, one she'd believed lost nearly a year ago. For an instant her head spun so she feared she might fall down. "How come you here? We thought you dead."

Catrin's eyes met hers in a look that combined raw desperation and pain. Her hands clung to Eadha's, and the guards—swaggering in their confidence—did not appear to take notice. "Not dead, nay, though mayhap 'twould be far better if I were. I have been here since they took me, and am slave to Harald, who oversees the chief's hall. I was claimed in a meeting much like this one." She glanced over her shoulder. "I saw you and the others brought in. I could scarce believe it! I need to warn you—"

"Claimed?" Eadha stared in horror. Aye, just as she and the other women had speculated, and feared.

Catrin pressed closer and whispered into Eadha's ear. "List, before my master recalls me. If you wish to survive this, you must be canny. Hear me? Do not look anyone in the eye. Try to appear weak and sickly—they do not like that. Do not let them know who you are. Or *what* you are. If they know you for daughter to a chief, 'twill increase your value, and you will likely be claimed by the Norse chief's son, him called Friti. He has already killed two wives and any number of slaves, the last in a fit of ire. Anyone who took part in the raids can claim you as reward. You do no' want it to be that beast."

Eadha, the lump of molten dread in her stomach turning to sickness, looked where Catrin indicated and, locating the man in question, blinked in dismay. She remembered him, aye—he had been at the forefront of the raid; her own father had faced him with a blade, and fallen.

Dead? Was her da truly dead?

Half smothered by terror and the sheer press of bodies around her, she fought to control the panic flooding her mind. Friti made a terrifying figure, and she did not want to imagine herself at his mercy. He stood now on a raised platform at the head of the hall beside another man who must be his father, the chief. Both big men, they wore fine cloaks over their leathers and held themselves like lords of the world. Aye, so, and lords they were, here in their own realm.

Catrin's fingers squeezed Eadha's painfully. "Try not to get chosen by him—or the berserker. Neither of them, understand? Pray on it."

And how was Eadha to manage that? Would prayers prevent such a thing? It seemed she had done nothing but pray since the long boats were first sighted off the shore of their settlement. Yet what other hope did she have? Sick with dread, she asked, "Which is the berserker?"

"There—in the great bearskin."

Ah, him. Eadha remembered him from the raid also—a whirling mass of hair and weapons, who spread blood wherever he went. Her gaze found him now where he leaned with deceptive calm against the wall at one side. Nay, nay, not him either. *Please, do not let me go to him.*

"He is mad entirely," Catrin said in a frantic whisper. "But do not worry, since I have been here he has never chosen a woman. He always asks for chattel instead."

"I *am* chattel." The words came through frozen lips. "They will no' want me." Eadha assured herself as much as Catrin. "I bear the mark." For most her life she had longed to be beautiful, like so many women of Clan Ewan, but she bore a brown birthmark on her right cheek. Now, for the first time, she felt glad of it.

Catrin looked doubtful. "These men care little enough for your face whilst plundering you in the dark."

Their little group shuffled to a halt. With a growl, a man appeared from the crowd, leaped forward, and roughly pulled Catrin away by the arm. Was that her master, that she called Harald? Would Catrin be punished for her kindness in trying to give Eadha warning? Och, aye, this must be a nightmare. But no, for even nightmares came to an end.

Laura Strickland

The chief, up on the dais, began to speak, and the noise level in the vast room dropped. The words he spouted meant little to Eadha; she could understand nothing. His tone, however, made of his speech an announcement, a boast tinged with self-congratulation. His boasting was met by more cheers, the intensity of which penetrated Eadha's flimsy defenses and made her shiver with apprehension.

Thank all the holy powers Catrin had managed to drop those few words into her ear and so prepare her for what must come. She clasped the hand of the woman closest to her—Morag, half a score years older than she, and with two bairns back home. Morag had not stopped weeping for her children since their journey began.

Would Morag, with her tangled hair and blotched, tearstained face, appeal to any of these savages? In truth, none of the Alban women could possibly look appealing at this point. Woefully battered by their passage through terror and over sea, clad in filthy tatters, she could not imagine even these savages wanting them.

Please, Lugh, she prayed desperately to the god of her heart—god of light—to whom she had long since given her devotion. *Deliver me from this cruelty. Deliver us all.*

Yet she saw how these men, with their long, fair hair and merciless eyes, already inspected her and her companions. She swayed on her feet a third time, and Morag's fingers tightened.

Courage. She had little courage left, though, and could not imagine anything beyond this moment—did not want to imagine being taken by force to some

6

stranger's bed.

The chief's loud diatribe went on and on. At Eadha's side, Morag once more began to weep, as did Rona, fourth down the line into which they had been nudged by a beast with a spear. Eadha wondered which of them would be first to collapse.

Yet it seemed other—perhaps lesser—chattel must be distributed first. The hall grew noisy again as goods stolen from Eadha's settlement were brought forth to be displayed and claimed—casks of fish, creels of grain, a small chest of silver that had belonged to Eadha's father, and even household items such as platters and cups. Shouts, challenges, and laughter rang out as the Norsemen contested over the spoils. At one point, a quarrel erupted and knives were drawn in what seemed a half-mock battle.

Lugh, I cannot survive in this place. Let me die now.

How much longer could she and her companions continue to stand awaiting their fates? It seemed they had been all but forgotten in the wild melee. But then the level of commotion suddenly dropped, and the chief, still on the dais, gestured at the woeful knot of women before speaking again.

Attention within the hall sharpened. Eadha, with her sensitivity to the emotions of others, felt it clearly, and her heart squeezed with pain.

The men who had participated in the raid—nearly two score of them—stepped forward, all but the one Catrin called a berserker, and the chief's son, Friti, who also remained on the dais. Perhaps they would not participate. Maybe she would at least escape those perils.

A crazed laugh rose to the back of her throat. All sense of safety had surely fled her existence. Anyway, the rest of this horde looked no better than those against whom Catrin had warned her, with their cold eyes and avid expressions, plundering her with their sharp gazes.

All six women held hands now in a desperate show of unity. The chief looked pointedly at the berserker, and Eadha held her breath until he shook his head decisively. One of the other Norsemen stepped closer, reached out, and captured wee Fiona's chin in his fingers. Eadha's stomach heaved in sympathy. Fiona—very bonny—would surely be the first chosen.

Fiona gasped, strove to pull away, and sank to the floor as her knees failed her. The line of women swayed and went down also; Eadha, at one end, fell to her knees.

"Up!" ordered the chief who, it seemed, possessed a few words of Gaelic.

Eadha struggled to stand. The warrior who gripped Fiona's chin in his fingers turned with a query to the chief's son, Friti. He, too, shook his head. The women began to wail loudly as Fiona was promptly hauled from their ranks.

Claimed as a prize. *Oh, Lugh, oh, Lugh...do not desert us, do not desert me.*

Hate surged through Eadha—not the first such wave she had felt since this horror began—and lent her the strength needed to help Morag up.

She glanced toward the dais and saw, in horror, the chief's son step down. Large and confident, his fur-trimmed cloak swirling about him, he approached at a deliberate swagger, his scarred face almost expressionless. The breath froze in Eadha's lungs as he strutted down the line.

Please, Lugh, she prayed again incoherently. But it did little good; the man paused directly in front of her and looked her in the eye. Too late she recalled Catrin's instructions: keep your head down, do not make eye contact with anyone. Now she'd been caught, and her breath suspended completely.

Cruel to his women, Catrin said he was—even more so than all the rest. And aye, Eadha could see that in his eyes, pale blue like a sky after the rain. He wore his wheaten-colored hair in a series of plaits, and he held his head with arrogance impossible to deny. Tall even by the standards of these giants, he towered over Eadha and her sisters.

Who had his last slave been, the one he had killed? Another captive seized somewhere else in Alba, or perhaps in Erin? What sort of brutality had brought about her death?

For he possessed a brutal face, and Eadha easily picked up on the emotions that filled him—an ugliness as casual as it was powerful. In his gaze, she found no hint of mercy. As had the other warrior, the one who had chosen Fiona, he seized her chin in one hand, and his large, rough thumb rubbed over the mark on her cheek. He spoke a word she could not understand. And in his eyes she saw…

No, no, no, no—she began a litany in her mind. She fashioned her terror into a force and pushed at him. *Not me, please, not me*.

But did she want him to choose one of her companions instead? As the daughter of their chief, did she not have a duty to take the worst of the punishment?

Perhaps, but…

Suddenly darkness, merciful darkness, flooded the edges of her vision. All she could see were the brute's eyes surrounded by a black cloud. Or perhaps she sensed his spirit.

The chief's son hauled her forward, away from Morag. The hall had now fallen silent, and in a guttural accent that slaughtered the Gaelic, he said, "To whom did you belong?"

The darkness lightened a bit as a hundred images flooded Eadha's mind. *To the sunlight dancing on the water and the waves caressing the shore, to my da with his loud laughter and ma with her gentle strength. To Lugh, Lugh, Lugh—*

"Answer," Friti demanded when she did not speak. "Had you a husband? Are you tried?"

Ah, so he wanted to plunder a virgin, this brute with his narrowed eyes and inherent cruelty—the man who just might have slaughtered her da.

Blindly, unable to find her voice, she nodded.

His face twisted in disgust. He said something in his own tongue and then repeated apparently for her benefit, "Spoiled goods!"

Cautious laughter traveled the room. Someone called something in return, and Friti made a gesture of negation.

Eadha's relief almost took her back to her knees. She had never lain with any man, but she would tell any untruth she must to survive.

Friti stepped away, and Eadha's relief flared. Just as she drew a breath, she caught movement from the corner of her eye.

The berserker. Horror froze her as she saw he had

stepped forward from his place by the wall, an act that caught not only Eadha's attention but that of everyone else in the room. A hush fell during which Eadha heard the loud tripping of her own heart.

Back home they had heard of these men—berserkers. Any Norse raiding party deserved fear and respect; one that included a berserker doubly so. The elite among warriors, they felt no pain and were unstoppable in battle. Madness seized them when they fought and sometimes when they did not.

Eadha had caught glimpses of this man in action during the attack on her home, and she shrank from him instinctively as he approached. Not Friti, so Catrin had said, and not the berserker. Yet how could she dictate who might claim her?

Lifting fearful eyes to the berserker's face, she found it contained no madness, at least not at the moment. Instead he looked quiet and composed. His eyes, trapped between brown lashes, were pale gray and clear as rainwater. One brow, dissected by a scar, sat askew. Other scars scored both cheeks. His hair, of light brown several shades darker than that of most his fellows, hung loose and straight down his back.

He gazed at Eadha intently but did not attempt to touch her. His gaze traveled from the top of her head—now a tangled mass of auburn brown—hesitated over the mark on her cheek, and moved to her bosom and on down.

Eadha began trembling anew, violently this time, not from his regard but from what she sensed inside him or rather did *not* sense—he held a complete void of emotion. Aye, she could tell much about those she encountered, often too much. But he...

Was it the berserker madness that blocked his emotions from her? Some spell of magic? Och, but she could not tell.

He spoke a single word Eadha failed to understand. The hall immediately went so still she could hear one of the women farther down the line sobbing softly. No one else so much as breathed.

The chief, in return, barked a question.

The berserker spoke the same word again as if in confirmation before turning his back and stalking off without another look.

The great hall broke up in chaos.

Chapter Two

Ended. The terrible, lengthy session in the great hall had ended at last, and Eadha found herself owned by someone. *Owned.*

Exhausted, stunned and shattered by the need to keep from weeping before them all, she barely noticed when Catrin slipped up and once more took her arm. The loud, dangerous, and terrifying warriors now left the hall in droves, passing them with barely a look. Eadha had apparently been forgotten, except by her friend.

"Come," Catrin said to her softly. Only one word, but Eadha heard the distress in Catrin's voice. "My master, Harald, says I may take you to your quarters, since the berserker has gone and left you behind."

Amid a crush of bodies, they filed out of the hall and into the surrounding darkness. The mad idea entered Eadha's mind: she could run—she could flee and possibly escape. She might make her way home…

The very word started such an ache in her chest, she thought she might die.

When they hit the open air, Catrin said, "I canna believe it. Did I not warn you to keep from getting chosen by the berserker? Oh, mercy, Eadha. Oh, mercy!"

"And how was I to do that—keep from getting chosen?" Eadha's voice sounded rusty when it came.

She jerked in her friend's grip and tried to look back at the hall. The other women had been claimed and their masters…new husbands?…had taken possession of them. Only she had been neglected.

"Where do you think he has gone?" she asked, hoping that perhaps the berserker, having thought better of it, did not want her after all. Surely his abandonment argued the hope.

"I know not," Catrin admitted unhappily. "To be sure, I did no' think there was any real danger of him claiming you. They win the order of right to choose by valor, you see—he usually gets first or second choice but has never claimed a woman and requests only valuables—silver or gold. Did you no' see the reaction back there? No one knows what to make of it."

Eadha peered more closely into Catrin's face. Above them, and to the north, the after-glories flickered in the sky, a show of majesty to which she could barely give her attention.

"Where do you take me, Catrin?"

"To his quarters. You are now his property."

Eadha drew a breath that seemed to scorch her lungs. "Tell me quick—what will be expected of me?" Would that brute, the monster who had spilled the blood of her clansmen, take her to his bed? Must she submit, or die?

And which, of those two, would she prefer?

Sympathy flooded Catrin's eyes. "You are his slave, with all the attendant duties, and must do as he dictates. Keep his dwelling and his hearth, answer every demand."

"Every?" Eadha's knees trembled harder.

"I am afraid so, lass."

"But I ha' never…"

"Aye, I ken." Catrin smoothed Eadha's tangled hair with gentle compassion. "And to have that madman be your first… Pray on it, Eadha. Pray hard."

No one could pray harder than Eadha already had. She'd sent nothing but a stream of prayers to Lugh since this ordeal began. What good came of it? Still the berserker had spoken for her.

"Catrin, I can sense nothing from him." Terrifying. "I do not understand why. 'Tis as if he is empty inside. I cannot endure a life spent in the power of such a man." She clutched Catrin's arm again and cast a desperate look around. "There must be some way to escape. No one watches us now." Incredibly, it was true. As soon as she'd passed into the berserker's possession, everyone else had lost interest in her.

"Is that what you think? There are eyes everywhere. Guards patrol this place, and even if they did not, there is nowhere to run. We are on an island, Eadha. That vast sea you crossed separates us from home."

"I do not care. To die in the wild would be better than—" Eadha's throat closed.

"They would hunt you down, and there would be punishment. I have seen. Like the rest of us, you need to concentrate on surviving. Be obedient and do not anger him. Then he may not beat you. Above all else, you do no' want to push this man into a rage."

Tears of terror clogged Eadha's throat, once more denying her speech.

Catrin hesitated before going on. "They say it becomes easier once the bairns come along. There is something for which to live, then." She splayed her free hand across her belly. "I am expecting now, though it does not show yet."

Eadha stared, not sure why the idea shocked her so.

Catrin went on in a whisper. "My master—he allows me to call him Harald—is twice my age. He first breeched me on the night he claimed me—there in the warriors' hall where others also sleep." She ducked her head. "Within hearing and sight of all."

Eadha did not know what to say. Back home, older men—widowers—did sometimes take young wives. But nothing, *nothing* here was like home.

She forced words through her tears. "How can you bear it?"

Catrin smiled grimly. "I do because I must. We women of Clan MacEwan are strong, are we not? Strong enough. Listen to me. You canna defy these men and you canna run. At least you were no' chosen by Friti, who has a score of complaints against him even from other men's wives. Come—courage!"

An echo of the voice Eadha had heard in her head. But that voice, like all her courage, had now flown.

****

"In a way, Eadha, you are fortunate. At least your master has demanded his own quarters and is valued enough by his chief to receive them," Catrin said as they passed through the doorway of the strange dwelling. "Others will not be witness to your humiliation."

Eadha made no reply. Back in Alba, buildings were made of native stone, part and parcel of the land. Eadha's father had raised a stout roundhouse upon their stretch of coast—one that had nevertheless failed to protect them from the menace that swooped in from beyond the horizon. Again and again they had been raided, and everything that could be seized had been taken.

She wondered once more if her father had survived that last raid. Her final glimpse of him had been the image of a strong man taken down, lying on the rocks in his own blood. If he had survived by some miracle, what would he—so valiant—expect from his daughter who had been stolen away?

This dwelling too looked as if it had sprung up from the native soil, but it had been constructed of turf, not stone. Green grass grew over the roof, and the side walls stood but knee high.

Just inside the entrance, Eadha balked.

"Come," Catrin bade. "As I say, at least you will be afforded some privacy and not despoiled in the warrior's hall like most of us, where everyone can hear—and see."

Aye, and was that the fate in store for the other women who had traveled here with Eadha?

Eadha did not feel fortunate, and her feet refused to take more than two steps inside the dwelling. The interior of the berserker's hut looked like a cave. It had no windows, and two deep slits, very low down, afforded access to what little remained of daylight. More light spilled in through the central smoke hole in the roof above a rectangular hearth. Dust motes swam in the beams cast by the gloaming, and the space evinced a powerful stink.

"Ugh," she said involuntarily.

Catrin gazed about. "What do you expect? Master Magnusson has lived alone a long while, with no one to look after him. You can at least make yourself useful cleaning and keeping his hearth. You wish to be useful—you do no' want to be a woman whose man tires of her and tosses her to his chief's warriors, as a…"

Catrin paused, apparently lacking the word. Eadha did not need to hear it.

Catrin resumed. "Women tend to avoid Master Magnussen, all but that Anaborg, who follows after him constantly. I ha' heard it said she has had every warrior here, save him."

Too much, Eadha's mind screamed at her. Too many things to fear and remember.

Yet Catrin went on. "I ken fine you ha' never been the sort of woman to tend a hearth or look after a man. Best begin now, if you want to survive." In the sifting light, Catrin's face looked grim. "Just make up your mind to it—there is no hope of happiness."

Eadha covered her face with her hands and, there beside what was to be her new hearth, sank to her knees in agony.

****

Tolljur Magnussen moved soundlessly through the soft, lingering light that colored the world. In his head he could still hear the roars of laughter and celebration that had rebounded in the great hall. He hated all of it— the posturing, the boasting, the recounting of feats in battle and the gloating over everything from the sharpness of one's axe to the seaworthiness of one's longship.

Tolljur made a face there in the hazy evening. Not a man for boasting, he would prefer to avoid the whole display if he could, and only attended at the insistence of his jarl.

Gunnar never failed to give Tolljur his due following a raid or battle. And that even though Gunnar's accursed son, Friti, made no secret of his belief that he should be declared their foremost warrior, with first choice of everything.

Tolljur wondered, not for the first time, if Gunnar did not fear him just a little. Friti, he knew all too well, did not.

Perhaps Friti should.

He hesitated when he saw the shaggy silhouette of his dwelling just ahead. What had made him act as he had this night? He'd quaffed no potion; the madness did not ride him. Instead, as he knew full well, he had followed impulse.

Ah, but that was something he did but seldom. Indeed, he could count the occasions on one hand. When not in his berserker's rage, he had his emotions always in hand. They fled him when he fought, along with the ability to perceive most sensations. He remembered taking none of the scars he carried. And he made a habit of refusing to feel sympathy for anyone.

Save the woman who had stood out in Gunnar's hall.

Why had she stood out? Even now, on his way to deal with the repercussions of the choice he'd made, he could not say. Yet he had held his breath from the time he saw her to the moment Friti took interest in her. Only when he'd stated his claim had he breathed again.

He could not let her fall into Friti's cruel hands. Not that she might fare any better in *his*. But at least he, Tolljur, might spare her, keep her from being hard used by others.

And, he asked himself as he approached his own

door, why should he care what befell the woman? Just another captive, so much chattel meant for working around the place and bearing sons.

Yet something about the expression in her eyes and—*ja*—the emotions he felt emanating from her, had made him act.

Fool, fool, fool, he chastened himself, even as he pushed open his door and went in.

What did he expect to see? The woman bending over his hearth, a cup of mead poured, his dwelling magically transformed from the grim pit he had made of it?

His gaze met with none of those things; instead he saw a cold hearth, an empty room, and dancing, filtered light.

Alarm touched him, and he cursed softly. Surely she had not run. Gunnar took such defiance poorly and expected his warriors to act upon it. She would be hunted mercilessly and punished without pity.

That made but one of the reasons Tolljur had never taken a slave—or a bride.

Cursing a second time, he reached into the cage beside the door and snatched a rush light. With flint from the pouch at his belt, he struck flame and narrowed his eyes against the flare.

The jumble that was his quarters met his gaze— weapons, discarded and filthy clothing, and other unnamed detritus sprawled everywhere, along with a puddle of spilled ale. The hearth had not seen fire in days, and despite the season, the interior of the dwelling felt dank, colder than outside.

It struck Tolljur he did not know her name, this female who had now become his property. He shut the door carefully and called softly in her tongue, "Woman?"

No response. His eyes, able to see so much, plundered the shadows that dodged the bars of light streaming in through the roof vent. He took a step forward and another. "I will not harm you."

Did he detect a movement in the far corner, the merest twitch among the shadows?

He took another step. "Come on out."

He felt it then—a shrinking of spirit as she tried to make herself invisible. A sigh escaped him. At least the worst had not happened; she had not run.

Evenly he addressed the corner. "Do not make me drag you out."

The shadows contracted more violently into themselves.

With a grunt, Tolljur approached the corner and held the frail light high. He saw her outline first; hunkered down and curled into a close bundle she was, arms wrapped about her knees and eyes shut tight.

He sought for words in his mind. He rarely communicated with slaves—or anyone—but could not have failed to pick up a sufficient amount of her language to get along. He tried to imagine how frightening it would be to find oneself captured and unable to so much as understand what was said.

"Arise. I will not harm you," he said again. "What is your name?"

Her eyes opened. Their whites caught a shine from the rush light in his hands. Slowly, moving like an old woman, she uncoiled herself and scrambled to her feet.

"Eadha. I am Eadha," she said.

Chapter Three

The man loomed over Eadha, shadows cast by the light in his hand making him look taller than he truly was. She had grown up surrounded by big men; her own father, chief Donnacht, possessed both height and breadth. The Norsemen she had so far encountered here used their size and bulk to intimidate.

This one made no exception. As she had in the hall, Eadha sought to plumb him with the inner sense that usually served her so well. Again she failed, meeting with only a baffling jumble of shadow and deeper darkness. Was it because he was a berserker? Or was it the fault of her terror? Her dread?

She did not like feeling intimidated and in the past had always held her head high. Daughter of a chieftain and graced by the gods—what had she to fear?

This—she feared this. That a man, a stranger, would now throw her down onto her back and wrest by force what she did not want to give.

Her heart pounded sickeningly, and she swayed where she stood, hands fisted at her sides. She resolved to fight, whatever the consequences.

And what if he went into the maddened state of the berserker when she resisted him...what then? Would he kill her in his rage?

Yet he continued to stand there with the light in his hand, with radiance washing over him, and failed to

22

move toward her. Peering at her with those pale eyes, he said, "I am Tolljur Magnussen. You call me Master Tolljur."

Master. The very suggestion of the word closed Eadha's throat. Wildly, she shook her head.

His pale eyes narrowed. Would it come now, the first blow? Would he see fit to beat her before he took her?

"Come. Sit."

His rough accent made an ugly thing of her beautiful language, that which she had always believed sang from the mouths of those she loved. She remembered times gathering kelp on the shore back home, hearing her friends and neighbors call to one another over the rocks, thinking it sounded less like speech and more like music. Yet he did not threaten, not now anyway. And she needed to survive, did she not? She drew a breath and nodded.

He gestured to a rug beside the hearth, and she huddled there, never taking her gaze from him.

To her surprise, he set about laying a fire in the hearth, busying himself in silence while stealing sidelong glances at her. When the flames leaped up, battling for dominance against the paler beams of gloaming, she could see the place—her new prison—better.

And see him better also.

He wore the same sort of clothing as all the Norse men—leather leggings covered to the knees by laced, leather boots, a woven tunic, gauntlets, and enough weapons to arm several ordinary men. Over it all he wore the shaggy, black-brown fur cloak which lent him such a feral quality. Eadha realized the bristling garment gave him additional bulk he did not actually possess. Big he was, aye, but much leaner than the chief's son, Friti, and surely not quite as tall.

His hair, a straight mane that reached his shoulder blades, looked golden brown in the leaping firelight; his angular face, nearly expressionless, was given a quizzical tilt by that scar which bisected the left eyebrow. The other scars that furrowed his cheeks perhaps explained why, unlike many of his fellows, he went clean shaven.

Once more, desperately, she sought inward knowledge of him, but his mind remained as closed as his expression. Did he guard himself from her? But why should he, when he knew nothing of her abilities?

She dropped her gaze to his hands and felt another shock. Broad-palmed and powerful, they bore more scars than unblemished skin.

He finished feeding the fire and snagged a jug left lying on its side amid the other rubble that littered the room. This he gave a shake and, satisfied, searched out a mug which he filled and brought to her.

"Here, drink."

Eadha accepted the cup, careful not to let her fingers touch his, and peered into it suspiciously. Ah— did he mean to dull her senses with drink so she might not resist him so fiercely?

He seated himself on a separate rug, where the fire cast light onto his face, making it look as if the scars there crawled and writhed.

Eadha's heart refused to calm, still beating so hard it turned her stomach. She cast a desperate look toward the door.

"Do not try and run," Tolljur said. "We would have

to hunt you down. I would be forced to punish you then."

Forced? Did he expect her to believe he might be loath to do so, this man against whom Catrin had warned her—the worst of all his kind?

In that calm, gravelly voice he went on, "Do not try to end your life, either. There are, here, many weapons lying about, *ja*?"

"End my life?" Eadha whispered, startled into speaking.

"Some try," he told her simply. "Most do not succeed but make dire wounds they yet survive."

Eadha, fingers cramped on the cup, said nothing.

"You will be missing your husband," he stated.

Husband?

Och, aye—she had told the chief's son she was despoiled. Would that untruth now cost her dear when this brute sought to rut with her as he might a woman used to accommodating a man?

The sickness rose into her throat, and she choked it back down.

"Have you *kinder* as well?" He seemed to seek for a word and asked carefully, "Bairns?"

"Nay."

"It is as well. Your name again? I am not sure I heard you."

"Eadha."

"A-dah." Carefully he repeated it. "Let me tell you what is expected of you. Be obedient. Keep the hearth and my clothing clean. Make this place tidy."

"What...what else?"

As he had in the hall, he inspected her, the pale gaze skipping from the top of her head to her cheek, where it paused. "Your face—what happened to it?"

She whispered, "Birth mark." Did he find her too marred, too ugly to take to his bed? Might she be so fortunate? If all she had to fear was his madness…perhaps she could survive after all.

Yet his examination continued down her body, lingering at her breasts. He hesitated before he said, "I require nothing more."

Ah—after that look, he must lie. Surely he omitted that other requirement, the most terrible among them all. Why would he speak for her if he did not intend to use her—this man who, so Catrin said, had never before taken a woman as a prize?

Perhaps he considered that act—accommodating him—a chore akin to sweeping the hearth, and not worth the mention.

The pale gaze returned to her face, and he added as if to make it clear, "I sleep there." He gestured to a pile of rugs against one wall, and Eadha tensed. He pointed to the corner where he had discovered her. "You make your bed there. I will not bother you."

All the breath escaped Eadha's body in a rush, leaving her so lightheaded she swayed where she sat.

Without thinking, she asked, "Why? Why did you speak for me if you do not intend—" She broke off, unable to voice what she feared most.

He hesitated once more, firelight leaping in his eyes. Suddenly he got to his feet and said dismissively, "Friti Gunnarssen would have taken you in the end, even if he played at not wanting you. He would have amused himself with you for a time and then thrown you to his pack of wolves." He turned to give her a long look. "Better with me."

Eadha held his gaze; cursed if she did not believe him.

Thank you, Lugh.

Chapter Four

The woman—Eadha—could not strictly be considered beautiful. But Tolljur had learned to shun beauty. Was not Anaborg Helmsdottir beautiful? And possessed of a black heart. He wanted no part of such a woman.

Truth be told, he wanted no part of this one either. He still did not know what had moved him in Gunnar's hall. Pity, maybe, or the sheer desire to thwart Friti. He certainly had not taken her out of lust—the fear of which he saw so clearly in her eyes.

He turned where he stood to survey her again. He could not seem to get his fill of looking. Ah, by Odin's eye, what a fool he was! Burdening himself with a woman, of all things, even out of pity, only further complicated his life.

He certainly did not need any more complications, though he had to admit his dwelling could use a good sweep and scrub. Would this Eadha be a competent and willing worker? Something about her declared her less than versed in things domestic, with a streak, perhaps, of the wild.

Ja, and that went to the heart of it, what he had sensed about her back in Gunnar's hall that made him speak out as never before.

Perhaps she would prove attractive, once clean and properly clothed. In the light of the hall, her tangled hair had carried a reddish gleam. Her face, with its sharp cheekbones, freckled skin, and that odd mark on the cheek, looked foreign enough to fire the passion of one such as Friti.

He, Tolljur, tended to pour all his passion into the madness when it took him.

What color were her eyes? He had not been able to tell in the hall and could not see them well enough now. Would she ruin them spending her time weeping and moping for her husband back in the islands? Had she the wit to accept her lot, safer here with him than elsewhere around Husavik?

He grimaced. For this very reason had he never taken a slave; he knew too well how it felt to be held captive to a higher power and forced to serve.

"This place," he waved a hand, "needs tending. I had a sister." He blanched at the thought. "She used to look after me, but she has been gone a long while."

Hate flared in his heart when he thought of Gyda's fate. While he could not in truth place her death at Friti's door, Odin himself could not make him consider the jarl's son innocent.

Eadha spoke, her voice rough with uncertainty. "You want me for a servant—just that?"

"I have time for nothing else. I am here seldom enough." He frowned. "Best for you to accept you cannot go home—ever."

What did he see in her eyes? Denial? Pain? Yet reality must be faced. He, better than anyone, knew that.

"You will begin your duties tomorrow. In the morning I will make provision for you—a bath, clothing. For tonight, take some rugs and sleep there."

He pointed again to the corner in case she had failed, still, to take his meaning.

Relief flooded her face at last. She set aside her cup, its contents untouched, and stared at him. "Thank you. I am grateful."

He shrugged awkwardly. "Do not give me any trouble and we shall get along well enough."

****

Huddled in her cache of blankets, Eadha lay listening to the sounds of the night and seeking the courage she would need to face the dawn. The journey on the longship had been terrifying, ridden by sickness and dread, but only now when she'd landed on her feet did the truth of her situation hit her.

It could be worse, she thought. And strove to believe in her fortune. She had been claimed by the feared berserker, and yet he said he did not want to use her harshly—to use her at all—and she believed him. Harder to believe she would never see her home again, would be forced to live out her days here among strangers. Never had she felt so alone.

Alone, aye, and yet not alone. She could hear her new master—the man who now owned her—breathing across the way. She could also hear footsteps and the voices of those passing outside, no doubt bound also to their beds. And she could hear the pounding of her own heart.

Help me, Lugh.

She had never been a woman of weak will. Sure of her place in the world and prepared to defy her father to seize the life she wanted, she'd not been easily cowed. Aye, her father had expected her to marry in order to benefit the clan and had not been pleased when she chose another course.

"What do you mean, you want to be a priestess?" he had bellowed when first she told him. "I want grandchildren, and for that you need a husband."

Eadha's mother, far more sympathetic, had sought to remonstrate with her husband. "Donnacht, she bears the mark, the one the gods put upon her at birth. And in this life we cannot choose our fates. She comes by this desire honestly; have there not been priests in this family back through history?"

Eadha's father, a warrior to the heart, glowered. "Priests. Priests! Men who chose a vocation. Not a woman—who, with her brothers dead, represents the sole chance to continue our line."

Yet Eadha, devoted to her god and what she believed to be her destiny, remained adamant. She had male cousins, two of them, who could follow her father in the succession. She believed herself meant to embrace the old ways, the faith of her ancestors that endured yet in the isles, even though much of mainland Alba had turned to Christianity.

Now, blinking into the dark of her new prison as the night moved toward morning, Eadha acknowledged she had always been different; even as a child she'd heard voices in the wind, seen pictures in the fire, understood the language of the seals, and believed the future might be told by a cast of stones. So she had pursued, with all her being, the path of devotion.

How had that benefited her in the end? Torn from the life she'd striven so hard to claim, she had lost everything, and her heart ached as never before.

Silently she asked Lugh, *Is this a just return for my arrogance, for my insistence, for my disobedience to*

Da? For I will, in the future, have no chance of disobedience.

Lugh did not answer, and fear of that proposed future made Eadha squeeze her eyes tight shut. She had been battered and beaten emotionally to the point where she'd attempted to hide in a corner from Tolljur Magnussen. Somehow she needed to gird up her courage and find a way to walk on, head high—slave or not.

And Tolljur Magnussen, this berserker who controlled her fate—what of him? She still could not understand why his emotions, which should be as clear to her as those of everyone else she encountered, remained cloaked.

Did he act out of mercy and kindness? But he had no reason to be kind. Did he hide some other motive she could not divine? How perilous was her existence, dependent on a stranger who could well trade her to another of these men.

His breathing, across the way, sounded even—he must sleep deeply. Again she gathered her spiritual resources and tried to plumb him, only to encounter the same wall—not of stone but of fog. Aye, he must keep himself hidden. But how did a man guard himself even in sleep?

He stirred suddenly, as if he felt her attempt to intrude upon him. Swiftly, she withdrew her attention. She did not wish to awaken him betimes. Moments alone in this new world would be precious, time in which she must seek to restore herself.

As for the future, she would have to wait and see what came to her with the new day.

Chapter Five

"So it is true."

Tolljur's head jerked up when his door flew open on its leather hinges, flooding the dwelling with dawn light. He knew that voice, and annoyance touched him even before he beheld the woman's form outlined in stark brilliance. She went on, "I swear I did not believe it. The great Tolljur Magnussen taking a slave."

"Anaborg," he growled. Had the woman no decency, bursting into a man's quarters at dawning? *Ja*, well, he knew she had no decency, this one—like a she-wolf on the prowl, she would venture anywhere.

"Where is she? I want to get a look at this creature you chose." Anaborg sashayed in, moving with the deliberate sensuality she wore like a fine cloak.

Tolljur slanted a look at Eadha, who had been caught poised on the far side of the hearth. Praise Odin she had not run while he slept. She looked hesitant and unhappy, though of course she could understand nothing Anaborg said.

As evenly as he could manage, he told Anaborg, "If you were curious, you should have been in the hall last night."

Anaborg shrugged. She wore her hair loose this morning, in a tumbled river of gold, her dress half unfastened across her generous bosom. Her eyes reached for Tolljur before she turned them on Eadha with dimming interest.

"I was otherwise engaged last evening. You and your fellows were away a long while raiding. A woman has needs."

Needs. Insatiable, the men called her behind her back and sometimes to her face. Tolljur knew her to be heedless and spiteful as well. She had ruined no less than three legitimate marriages—and laughed about it after.

And all this in pursuit of her desire to lie with every warrior who fought beneath Gunnar's banner. She had not yet lain with Tolljur and would not. He would throttle her first.

Not but he had to admit she was beautiful. Even now, fresh from some other man's bed, she looked bewitching, the lush curves beneath her clothing making promises Tolljur believed she would eagerly keep.

He had seen her naked once when, like now, she came pushing in here and disrobed for him. He'd also heard the stories from his fellow warriors about the acts she performed in bed—and out of it.

Now her gaze plundered Eadha, who stood in her soiled rags, the contrast between them ludicrous. Anaborg tossed her head. "That? She is not even beautiful. And she is blemished."

Again Tolljur shot Eadha a look, glad she could not understand. Anaborg rounded the hearth and drew closer to the captive, who withdrew a step.

"You told me you did not want a woman. Why this one? Why now?"

The very questions Tolljur had asked himself without answer.

"Be gone, Anaborg. Nothing here concerns you."

"Oh, but it does." Anaborg turned upon him eyes bright with curiosity and blue as the far sea. "You are meant to be mine."

"I am not."

She veered course, abandoning any interest in Eadha to approach him instead. "*Ja,* I have always known you are the man—the one man—who could satisfy me." Her lips parted. "I want you in a rage. Rough as you like."

She already bore bruises on the white skin at her throat and lower down. Who had inflicted them? Could she imagine he would want another man's leavings? He shuddered inwardly.

Starkly he said, "I am not interested. I have chosen a woman for my hut. Let it end with that."

"Do not tell me you truly intend to take her to your bed? You are wasted on her, Tolljur."

Tolljur shrugged. The impulse that had moved him to claim Eadha went beyond intention.

Anaborg widened her eyes at him. "Even so, it does not mean we cannot lie together. I have never let another woman—slave or otherwise—deter me."

"I assure you I have no desire to lie with one woman and betray her with another."

Anaborg laughed. "You are mad; it is what all men desire. And I am surprised. Your madness has never before spilled over from the battlefield. You told me you did not experience lust, Tolljur. That all your passion burned away in the fighting fit."

True. When it came, it scoured him—a far more merciless mistress even than Anaborg might prove.

"Go," he said again. "Leave me to my life." Such

as it was—bleak and dark, lit by intermittent flame.

She stalked her way around to his side of the hearth and paused, her demanding gaze fixed on his face. She lifted one hand and traced the scars on his left cheek with a finger. He had to stiffen in order to keep from recoiling.

"This is not over, Tolljur Magnussen," she whispered. "I will yet lie with you."

He seized her wrist in his fingers. He knew his grip could fracture bone. Not the tallest or bulkiest of Gunnar's men, his strength had been honed by the excesses to which the madness pushed him. His appearance, as he well knew, belied his savagery.

Anaborg did not flinch; instead her expression became enraptured.

Very softly, even though he knew Eadha could not understand the words, he said, "I have warned you not to touch me." He released her with a shove.

"It seems your new slave is destined for many lonely nights." Anaborg's gaze skipped down Tolljur's body. "A pity." She turned at last to the open doorway, where she paused again and flung a look at Eadha. "But what more does a filthy Alban woman deserve?"

Tolljur growled wordlessly as she stepped out into the sunlight. Hands fisted, he shoved the door shut with his hip, and returned the interior of the hut to its customary gloom.

Shooting a look of his own at Eadha, he wondered if he should try and explain Anaborg's intrusion. In truth, as his slave she warranted no explanation—she would be expected to do as bidden and put up with whatever occurred between these walls. But she would undoubtedly encounter Anaborg again and thus needed some warning.

"Sit." He accompanied the words with a gesture, and she sank down beside the now-cold hearth. Carefully, he spoke in Eadha's tongue. "That woman is called Anaborg Helmsdottir. You will stay well clear of her."

Eadha's gaze traveled to the door. Tolljur realized he still did not know their true color. He chastised himself; what mattered the color of a slave's eyes?

Eadha nodded.

"Today, as I have said, I will make provision for you—clothing, a bath." He glanced around the room. "You will clean and tidy this place. Have you any questions?"

She laced her fingers together in her lap and spoke but one word. "Midden?"

Ah, *ja*, that. Tolljur's own bladder felt ready to burst after all the ale taken in the hall last night. By Odin's ravens, he had become so used to living alone he never thought about pissing in the pot that occupied the corner behind the door—nor emptying it on a regular basis. No wonder the place stank.

"Come, I will show you," he said.

****

Out in the bright sunlight, Eadha found the settlement already well astir, folk hurrying about, calling to one another in greeting. She paused involuntarily to take in the lie of the land in this new and foreign place.

The settlement faced northward, unlike hers in Harris, which faced roughly west. But the sea—source of so much joy to her, always—still made its presence known. Just below the clustered buildings lay a sheltered bay, its arms stretched toward the infinity of a milky blue horizon. The rising sun rode far to the east. To get home, she would have to sail north out of the bay, then follow that sun and steer south, in the direction of Alba.

Three great longships—the fleet in which Eadha had arrived—floated on the still water, along with many smaller vessels. The land slanted upward gently from the harbor, all gray and bright mossy green, nearly treeless. Here and there about the settlement had been constructed pens, mostly built of stone, where she saw goats, sheep, and geese. A few ponies wandered about like common residents. Spread out on either side of the dwellings were neat fields, green with growing grain.

Tolljur's dwelling stood about halfway up the rise; behind it, the terrain climbed still higher to a rolling summit topped with rock. Despite the improvements the residents had made, the place seemed nearly featureless after the beauty of Harris. How did these people survive?

"Come," Tolljur repeated, and she jerked back into motion. He went several steps ahead of her and carried the stinking pot in which she supposed she would be expected to relieve herself in future. Must she share it with him? Unprepared for such intimacies, she grimaced.

He led her down the slope, between other dwellings and away to the right of the harbor, where lay the midden—not so different from similar accommodations with which she was familiar—and turned away to unfasten his clothing while she did as she must. Other folk there, a goodly handful of them, greeted Tolljur cautiously and shot curious looks at her even as she smoothed her tattered skirt back down.

She could understand nothing they said, but—unlike with her new master—she easily picked up their emotions, a blend of curiosity, hesitance, and approbation. Though these people clearly respected Tolljur Magnussen, they did not seem eager to interact with him. His fellow warriors appeared most at ease, yet even they held back, wariness in their eyes.

None went so far as to question him about her presence, as had the woman who'd crashed into the hut earlier. Eadha had no need to understand Anaborg's words to tell what she'd been about. She wondered what Anaborg meant to Tolljur and if they played at some lovers' game. The woman was certainly beautiful enough—and bold enough—to snare any man's attention. And Eadha understood nothing of the customs in this place.

She hoped Anaborg had indeed claimed Tolljur's affections. Then she, Eadha, need not fear him expanding her duties to include something she could not bear to contemplate.

They headed back to the dwelling, Tolljur now carrying the empty pot and Eadha still at his back, and Tolljur hailed a passing woman.

Of middle years, the woman had a broad, sturdy form and wore her hair under a cloth wound tightly around her head. She shot Tolljur an interested look and directed another sharper one at Eadha before propping the basket she carried on her hip. She and Tolljur began a conversation, which to Eadha sounded like so much jabbering.

Eadha occupied herself with probing the woman's emotions instead—reading the spirit, the old shaman back home called it when she confessed her ability to him.

"Not many possess that talent, lass," he'd told her in a voice cracked with age yet still melodious. "Not many would want it now, with the new religion creeping across the land. Guard it well. In the old days—the days of our glory—you would have been born a priestess."

"That is what I hope to be." Eadha gazed into his eyes and lifted her chin. "I care not for the new religion. I want to live as you do."

"Ah, lass, but I am old, and part of the order passing away. Would you choose a life of sacrifice?"

"Aye."

"Devoted only to your gods?"

Lugh would bring her all the comfort she needed. Did she not hear his voice in the waves and catch the glint of his spear in the lightning?

"It is a lonely road, lass."

Ah, but old Neal knew nothing of loneliness, Eadha thought bitterly while she waited for Tolljur to conclude his business with the woman. It fairly consumed her, here.

The woman abruptly switched her gaze back to Eadha and spoke in her tongue, apparently for her benefit.

"*Ja*, Tolljur, I will take her in hand as you ask and help her learn. Begin by giving her the pot to carry. She is meant to be your servant, not the other way round. What will folk think?"

Tolljur shrugged, the movement signifying his indifference to the opinions of others, but he passed the malodorous pot into Eadha's hands.

The woman smiled tightly. "I am Inger, who was friend to Tolljur's mother. He has asked me to take you under my wing, which I will do. You, Tolljur, go and get your breakfast. Leave us."

Tolljur nodded and stalked off without a backward glance.

Inger fixed Eadha with a hard eye. "Come along, then. We will try and make something useful of this blunder."

Chapter Six

Inger possessed a fair command of Eadha's tongue and proved not loath to speak. All the way back to Tolljur's hut she barked instructions.

"You will keep his hearth swept, his clothing brushed, his room tidy, and answer his every command. You will put his comfort ahead of your own, always. Early or late, it will not be too much trouble to serve him. If his weapons need polishing, you will do it. If his wounds need binding, you will tend them. He has become your reason for living. Do you understand?"

Eadha, bristling inwardly, said nothing. As daughter of a chief and a fledgling priestess, she'd never taken orders from anyone save Lugh. It stuck in her craw to agree to this.

At the door of Tolljur's hut, Inger paused and glared at her. "Do you understand? It shall be much the worse for you otherwise. Punishment here comes swift and hard."

"Punishment?" Tolljur had mentioned that also, last night.

"See how many slaves carry stripes beneath their clothing and then tell me how you relish disobedience. Me, I have broken in more slaves than I care to number. I know the way of it. Did Tolljur warn you not to run?"

Eadha nodded.

"Heed him well. The jarl's son, Friti Gunnarssen,

loves nothing better than to order punishment for those who flee, especially females. He will have you naked in front of the company before you can beg for mercy." She planted her hand on the door of the hut. "Do not be stupid."

"Nay."

Inger shoved the door open and promptly shied at what she saw—and smelled. "By Thor's beard, this place is a midden. You will work hard."

Eadha followed the woman in and paused when she barked, "Prop the door wide. Get as much light and air in here as possible. Ah—does the man even own a broom?"

As Catrin had already pointed out, Eadha possessed little inclination toward things domestic— weaving, cleaning, or cooking. At home such things had been done for her, and she'd spent much of her time out on the shore or playing her harp.

Fingers skilled on harp strings, however, proved clumsy beneath Inger's direction. Merciless, the woman barked commands and prodded Eadha into compliance, apparently heedless of the passing time. Under her direction, Eadha sorted, bundled, and hauled countless objects outside. Rugs were shaken, garments hung, and the floor swept, all while the sun traveled across the clear blue sky. Passing people paused to stare before moving on again.

More than once, as the day crawled by, Eadha thought of Tolljur, sent away to his breakfast so long ago. She had been offered not so much as a cup of water and eventually swayed on her feet.

When all the trash had been carried from the dwelling, a new fire laid, and the other goods organized, Inger paused and raked Eadha with a sharp eye.

"What is the matter with you that a bit of work turns your cheek pale? Wait here."

The woman, who had worked at least as hard as Eadha yet appeared tireless, stalked off with her arms akimbo. Eadha, half-dazed, stood outside in the gentle sunlight and once more let her gaze wander down to the bay in longing. The way home. If only she could throw herself into the salt sea and swim like a seal, transform herself into a kelpie, leave all this pain and strife. *Help me, Lugh.*

She became aware that people still stared, and ducked back inside. Difficult to warrant the change in the place, she admitted.

Dust motes still swam in the air—product of all the sweeping—but the new rushes Inger had spread smelled sweet, and the hut looked tidy. On the right, Tolljur's wooden bed had been piled high with clean rugs. A similar stand had been erected on the other wall, near where Eadha had slept last night. Inger had not asked about their sleeping arrangements, just grunted when Eadha told her where she'd spent the night.

All this while they had not seen Tolljur. Where might he be? Off training at arms? Yet surely he had left all his weapons behind, more weapons than Eadha imagined one man could ever use. She and Inger had lined them up, hanging most on the low beams near his bed. Later, said Inger, when time afforded, Eadha would polish them. Some were dull, their edges chipped, as she'd noticed when she handled them. Others, like the great axe which she could barely lift, bore splashes of what could only be blood.

Oh, Lugh, were these the same weapons used against my own people? Could that be my da's blood I see? In what terrible dream have I landed?

And should she, Eadha, appropriate one of these dire tools? Secret it about her person as a means of defense? A small knife, perhaps. And, were she discovered with it, what might the punishment be?

No time. The movement of a shadow behind let her know Inger had returned. The woman bore a cask of clear water and two small loaves of new-baked bread.

"Here. Eat and drink before we carry on."

Eadha accepted the food gratefully. "Surely we are done?"

"With the dwelling, *ja*. Next we begin on you."

****

In a sour mood, Tolljur made his way homeward. Already the moon rose into the arch of a sky that, at this time of year, saw little real darkness. Restlessness and dissatisfaction stirred together inside him. Just back from a raid and already he chafed at staying put. Not that he enjoyed raiding nor, in truth, battle of any kind. Difficult to enjoy what one did not remember.

Ja, he recalled parts of a journey: the sea voyage, arming himself, and going ashore. He recalled first sighting their target and choosing his opponent. After that, it became all fire and darkness—bright darkness, if he could warrant such a thing. When the madness took him, it took him completely. He heeded no injuries and felt no pain. Only when he came to after did he feel the sting—and that, too, he remembered.

But he did not get his wounds treated as did ordinary men, at least not at the outset. He could not be seen to bear injury like the others. While away at viking, his wounds were dressed perfunctorily by the slave Tiff, and once at home he went to Gunnar's shaman for tending, as for the potions that saturated his life.

His mouth curled in a bitter smile as he approached his own door. He'd just now come from the old shaman, Kaddi Haraldssen, who might be considered his only friend. After Kaddi tended his wounds, Tolljur had hoped to speak to him about Eadha. But others had arrived and come pushing in, asking Kaddi about augurs for future battles, and had then begun riding Tolljur about his new slave, so he left.

He wondered how Inger had made out training the woman, pushed open his door, and stared.

For one mad instant he wondered if he had entered the wrong house. These could not be his quarters that smelled so sweet, glowed with the light of a good fire in the hearth, and lacked a jumble of discarded clothing and weapons.

What was more, beside the hearth stood the great wooden tub he sometimes used to bathe his wounds away from the eyes of others, and in the tub...

It took him a full twenty heartbeats to realize it must be the same woman, the one he had claimed last night. Submerged in the water, her hair already washed and streaming wet, she sat with soap foaming around her breasts, both of which he could just glimpse. Inger stood over her, a rough cloth in her hand, and both women raised startled faces to him.

Ja, and Inger had promised to make his new slave neat and presentable, like his quarters. He had returned too soon. Who would think it would take so long?

Perhaps he should retreat. Yet he had been taught all his life a man never retreated from his own hut. Here he was king, with rights to everything.

Except this woman. He had promised her—and himself—he would not make use of her as other men did their female slaves. He had little in common with other men.

Beholding her now, however, made him regret giving the promise. He still did not find her face with its stark lines and prominent cheekbones particularly appealing. Her hair, though, was beautiful, a thick curtain of brown, gleaming with red in the firelight. Her skin, pale as the foam on the ocean yet marked generously by those freckles, made his eyes narrow. Her breasts…

He caught himself there, hauling back hard on his thoughts, but his eyes could not stop looking. Perfect those breasts were, the right size to fit into his hands and enticingly freckled, the nipples just breaking the surface of the water.

For the first time in recent memory he became aroused, his manhood growing thick and heavy against the leather leggings.

In defense he turned his gaze on Inger and said in his own tongue, "I thought you would be done."

Stridently she returned, "There was much work here. You lived in a midden."

"Surely not so bad as that." For the life of him, Tolljur still could not keep his gaze from returning to the woman in the tub, even though decency bade otherwise. He could see the outline of her slender body beneath the water, white knees drawn up. The curtain of her hair shielded her shoulders, and even as he stared she brought up both arms to cover her bosom.

With all his being he wished she would stand up so he could see the rest of her.

Inger gave a tight smile and, just as if she saw inside his mind, told the woman in Gaelic, "Get up and out now; we are done here."

Eadha shot a disbelieving look at her. "But—"

"Your master is home, and your first consideration is to serve him. What have I been telling you all day long?"

Eadha turned a speaking look of protest on Tolljur. She did not need to use words when she could communicate so clearly with a glance.

He remembered what he had seen earlier—much earlier—when he'd escorted her through the settlement to the midden: the color of her eyes in the bright sunlight. Mossy green mixed with brown they were, the peaty hue of the pools in her own land. Not one color but a mix of them—a mystery just like his reason for claiming her.

Now courtesy once more demanded he should look away, but he could not and stood watching while she rose to her feet in the wooden tub, eyes not modestly downcast but stabbing a glare back at him.

She possessed defiance, a bad thing in a slave but just possibly fine in a woman.

Inger handed her a cloth with which to cover herself, talking all the while as if she saw nothing unusual about the situation. "Well, what do you think of your quarters? I hope you are impressed. It took the whole day, and I worked as hard as your slave."

"You are a good woman, Inger."

"Now the place and your slave both smell sweet."

Inger's blue eyes snapped at Tolljur. "You can use both as you will."

With an effort, Tolljur withdrew his gaze at last from Eadha. She had turned her back to him while she wrapped herself in the cloth, affording him a tantalizing view of her wet hair spilling all the way down past her buttocks.

"There will be none of that," he told Inger harshly.

"Why not?"

"You know why not."

Eadha cast him a questioning look over her shoulder. She might not understand his words, but she comprehended the tone.

"Go." Inger spoke in Eadha's tongue and gave her a push. "Dress yourself."

Eadha stepped from the tub, once more engaging all Tolljur's attention. She went to the corner, where a new bed had been erected. Again, he tore his gaze away.

Inger smiled again. "A blind fool could see you want the woman."

"Hush."

"Why? She cannot understand. Anyway, it is her duty, if you would have it."

Tolljur thought about that. The woman—this woman—for his bed, obedient to his every command. Only he did not want obedience. He shook his head.

"I will stay for supper," Inger decided. "We will talk further of this."

Chapter Seven

Eadha bent low and offered Tolljur the platter. Her hair fell over her shoulder and she flung it back again, all too aware he watched her from the corner of his eye—still. Once more she tried to plumb his emotions with the ability that usually served her so well, and failed.

She did sense a change in him since he'd returned to find the dwelling all tidied and the fire lit. But it made him no easier to measure.

Inger, on the other hand, fairly battered the room with her emotions, as she had all the day long. Her feelings toward Tolljur, strong and maternal, nevertheless held a hint of respect or restraint—Eadha could not tell which. And the woman rarely stopped talking long enough for Eadha to plumb her.

At least now, after a stern glare from Tolljur, she spoke in Eadha's tongue, so Eadha could follow the conversation, most likely because she discussed Eadha herself.

"You might have made a better choice, Tolljur, had you acted on something besides impulse after all these years. This one is woefully lacking in skills. About the only thing she can do properly is lay a fire. Would you believe I had to teach her how to sweep? And only look at those cakes she made."

Compliantly, Tolljur bent his gaze on the platter,

and Eadha winced. She had to admit the griddle cakes looked a mess. Indeed, she had seen them prepared hundreds of times back home—the ingredients Inger provided her did not seem so different. Yet the sticky dough had clung to her fingers, and the result could only be considered a failure.

"I ask you," Inger went on angrily, "what kind of woman cannot do the simplest of chores? What slave wastes her master's precious supplies? You could not have chosen worse."

Tolljur raised his pale eyes from the platter to Eadha's face. Close to him as she was, she could see the depth of the scars that raked his cheeks and the golden stubble that dotted the skin between. Sudden awareness of him touched her—not an inner sensing but the physical kind.

"Serve your master, girl," Inger snapped. "Tolljur, it will take months for this one to learn her place."

"I am content," Tolljur said.

"Well, I am not. Girl—Eadha—what was your station at home, that you do not know how to sweep a floor?"

Eadha, having shoveled several cakes into Tolljur's hands, straightened. Catrin had warned her not to reveal the importance of her place in her father's house. Yet she had to give some believable answer, even if only another lie.

"I—uh—my father remarried. His wife wished to do everything herself and taught me nothing."

Inger grunted, a clear expression of her disdain. "Did you not keep your own hearth? Rumor has it you were married."

Were married, Eadha repeated to herself bitterly—

51

just as if her life and all it held in the past had ended. Which it had, in truth.

Pain tore through her. Tolljur met her gaze and said something briefly to Inger in Norse.

The woman barked, "Do not coddle her, Tolljur—I warn you it will end badly. She must accept her place here. You are not usually a soft man; do not begin now."

Before Tolljur could speak, Inger turned back to Eadha. "How long were you wed?"

"Only a few months. Since winter." In winter the raids from the sea subsided; it made the only time couples could think of other matters.

Inger grunted. "A newlywed. Makes sense. Her man would have had her on her back most of the time."

"Enough," Tolljur snapped, and the look he cast at Eadha carried a hint of sympathy. "She will learn our ways in time."

"She will have no choice." Mercifully, Inger then moved on to other topics, speaking of the raids just past and inquiring as to when the warriors would leave again.

Eadha's ears perked up at that. When finished serving, she unthinkingly took a seat near the hearth, though Inger grunted at her again. What did that mean? That Eadha, too lowly to sit in the presence of her master, should instead stand or wait behind him?

But Tolljur said nothing, and Eadha stayed where she was, striving to glean something to her benefit.

Inger spoke at length, occasionally lapsing into her own tongue if she lacked sufficient vocabulary to express what she wished to say. Tolljur's replies always steered her back into Gaelic again.

Eadha had no idea how unusual it might be for a Norse laird to afford a slave such courtesy; she concentrated on learning what she could.

It being barely midsummer, the Norse lairds would be raiding for many weeks yet. Since her new master was a vital part of the fighting force, she could expect him to be away much of the time.

To her surprise, she also learned—when Inger questioned Tolljur about it—he had returned from this past venture bearing wounds. She had seen no evidence of them, and even under Inger's bullying he refused to say how badly injured he might be. He admitted he'd been to see someone called Kaddi and had the worst of them tended.

This sent Inger on another tirade, mostly in her own tongue, some in Eadha's. "He is no fit healer, Kaddi. He may do well enough tending you in other matters, but you should see someone with proper skill in healing."

Tolljur listened to her with no perceptible reaction within or without, consuming Eadha's messy cakes stoically, and Inger's advice with them.

At last, as the gloaming settled into place outside, the woman got to her feet. "I must go. My own servants need direction." She glared at Eadha. "Tolljur, I hope you discover something this one is good at. Girl, have you absolutely no abilities?"

Staring, Eadha retorted, "I can play the clairsach."

"Clairsach? That is a harp?" Inger seemed taken aback. "Music, eh?" She directed a sharp look at Tolljur. "Did you know? Is that why you chose her?"

He gave a shake of his head, not looking at Eadha.

"Well, girl," said Inger surprisingly, "you may yet

prove of some worth."

And what did that mean? Eadha wondered as she watched the woman go through the door. Frustration rose inside her, along with weariness; she understood so little and felt constantly bewildered.

What difference could it possibly make if she could play music? Was that a skill much valued here among these marauders?

She wanted to ask Tolljur, as she longed to ask so many things. Difficult as it was for her to sense his emotions, she yet perceived no deliberate cruelty in him as in Friti, the chief's son.

Yet Inger had spent much of the past day lecturing her about paying respect to her master, which included not speaking until spoken to, and so she said nothing.

The silence drew out between them even as the light in the room faded. How was she to live with this man in subjugation—in silence—the rest of her days?

Lugh, help me!

If Lugh might come from the sea all clothed in silver like foam touched by moonlight, what would he say? *Accept your place for the time. Harbor your strength. Keep your weapons to hand.*

But she had no weapons save her wit and her faith. And her tongue.

"May I ask you a question?" Her voice broke the silence, hoarse as the croak of a raven.

Tolljur looked startled, as if he'd been in a world of his own. His impassive expression neither encouraged nor forbade her, but he said, "Speak, Eadha."

"You are a powerful man among your people, aye? An important man."

That seemed to surprise him. The bisected eyebrow

twitched.

When he failed to speak, Eadha pressed, "Foremost among these warriors."

Aye, and that must stick in the craw of that brute, Friti. No wonder she'd sensed tension between them.

She arose from her place beside the hearth and approached Tolljur. When near enough to touch him, she knelt at his side.

"You will then have influence with your chief. You could send me home if you chose. We could deal together—bargain."

He inspected her slowly from her hair to her knees, his eyes empty of all but regret.

"With what might you bargain?"

"I will find something. Something you value more than my presence. Your friend is right—I am a woeful excuse for a servant, and I do not doubt you would be happier still on your own. Your people engage in trade, aye? Trade me for something better."

"Such as?"

"What do you want?"

He gazed directly into her eyes as if he weighed and assessed her—not her outward appearance but her spirit. How strange it would be if he could divine her the way she could divine others, and him the only person she could not measure.

"Nothing you can give me."

"Do not be so sure."

Emotion stirred in his eyes, so empty but a moment before. He leaned toward her, and she caught his scent, clean and woodsy, with a hint of animal.

"Can you afford me release from this curse that consumes me?"

The words, bitter and ironic, invited no real answer.

Eadha dared to ask, "The madness, you mean? The berserker fits?"

His lips twisted, and the firelight glinted in his clear, silver eyes. "I am a prisoner you see, Eadha, even as you are. Find a way to free me, and I will gift you your freedom also. So I do vow."

Chapter Eight

Tolljur eased the clean tunic down over his body, wincing involuntarily as his wounds pinched and stretched with the movement. He wondered how long it would take him to heal this time. The old shaman, Kaddi, to whom he'd gone for tending, had given him rough care, along with another of his vile potions, purportedly for strength.

Tolljur did not feel much better as yet. A recurring test of his endurance it was, coming out of the madness to find himself—as ever—marked by wounds he did not remember taking.

When in the berserker state he felt neither the kiss of the sword or the sting of the knife. Likewise, fire could not halt him. Only a blow from a cudgel could knock him senseless and still the madness within him. And very few, faced with his fury, had the courage or opportunity to club him down.

If he felt no wounds during battle or contest, he certainly experienced them in full after.

Kaddi, the one-eyed shaman who had tended Tolljur's father before him, advised stoicism.

"Bear it like a bear," he often chided, his lips curling in a rueful smile. "Like the bear you become, boy. Never let them see your pain. That is part of the mystery, see, that makes you what you are."

Tolljur cared little for mystery. He still

remembered his father after a battle. Once emerged from the trance, he would suffer and groan, curse his pain, all beneath the hands of Tolljur's mother. Tolljur had inherited his father's bear cloak after his father's death when Tolljur was only twelve, along with his madness.

What did he remember most from that time? His sister's grief, his mother's devastation, his father's release. *Ja*, death brought release from the madness, yet for a berserker, death was hard to achieve.

He recalled also the honor paid his father at his funeral and Kaddi—not quite so old then—coming to Tolljur after, placing his father's bear cloak on his shoulders, and saying, "You will take his place now—and accept his burden."

Tolljur's mother had wept for days, inconsolable. She had followed her husband into death not ten months later, leaving Tolljur to protect his sister alone.

At which task he had failed.

He paused now in the act of dressing, pierced by the bright sunlight coming in through the smoke hole over his head. He could not blame his mother for following his father—such had their love been despite his father's affliction. His *modir* had known what their life would be when she took him to husband. She'd adored him in spite of it, each and every day they shared.

So despite what Tolljur believed, it was possible for one such as him to find love—however briefly—in this harsh existence. Always, in the back of his mind, had he carried that knowledge, sure he would settle for nothing less.

That, or nothing at all.

He remained just as certain he would not bring into this world a child—a son—afflicted like himself. That, he believed, had hurt his mother as much as anything else, knowing her son would suffer the same hard life as her husband.

That had not stopped her abandoning Tolljur and Gyda to follow her love.

He straightened his body with a groan, and his thoughts flicked to Eadha—he did not know why. He had sent the woman to fetch water, a customary early morning duty of all servants. She should have been back by now.

Upon that thought his ear caught the sound of a sudden ruckus carried up the slope from the direction of the harbor; shouting and a general clamor. Why he should connect it with Eadha, he could not say. Yet he moved to the door of the hut and looked out.

Surely the girl would not attempt to run. He had warned her, and anyway, she had seemed calmer last night after they made their agreement.

He cursed himself, wondering why he'd granted her such a bargain—one did not bargain with slaves, and she could not free him even if she wanted to. If his mother's love could not free his father, then nothing on earth could free him, Tolljur.

The new sun, riding far to the east, reflected off the water of the bay and half blinded him as he leaned out. But he caught a flash of color and what sounded like a scream from the direction of the pool where the settlement procured its water, and he caught up his knife from beside the door before dashing out.

Whatever occurred, he expected to find Eadha at the center of it, and his quick, assessing gaze did just that. A crowd had gathered beside the pool, mostly servants with jars and other vessels. His stomach tightened when he saw Eadha standing like a she-wolf at bay, armed only with the large jug from his dwelling, and a second woman sprawled on the ground behind her.

And facing them, at the head of his group of friends—who else but Friti Gunnarssen, wearing an ugly leer on his face?

Ja, Tolljur knew how it went: Friti and his companions drank most of the night and wandered the settlement causing trouble where they could, often sharing one woman among them and appropriating other men's slaves as they chose. Folk in the settlement frowned upon the practice—no one wanted a slave with another man's brat in her belly. But few defied the jarl's son.

Tolljur's quick assessment gleaned it all: the girl sprawled on the ground—a newcomer—must be a member of Eadha's clan from back home, and Eadha had stood to protect her. Despite his thoughts, he called as he hurried up, "What goes on here?"

A score of faces turned toward him. Rage flared in Friti's eyes. And what did Tolljur see in Eadha's face? Could it be relief?

Friti spoke in the confident bark that never failed to set Tolljur's teeth on edge. "Your slave is defiant, Tolljur Magnussen, and needs to be taught a lesson. If you do not teach her, I will."

"Touch a hair of her," Tolljur pronounced in return, "and I will tear you apart."

To be sure, he could feel the madness building, simmering inside him like the first dancing bubbles when water comes to a boil. Darkness gathered at the edges of his vision, all shot through with streaks of red fire, and he could no longer feel the knife in his hand.

Friti should have taken warning. A berserker did not enter the fit only during battle or after a potion. Honest anger could trip it also, though Tolljur rarely displayed that, or indeed any emotion.

Perhaps that made Friti incautious enough to taunt him now, to sneer and say, "You mean like this?"

Swift as a viper he seized Eadha by the hair and swung her hard, the force of it tearing a cry from the girl and knocking her off her feet. Tolljur's response came instantly and from a place he had trained himself to disregard—his heart.

And then the beautiful morning broke up into shards of red.

****

Pain, terror—screaming—and the flash of bright metal all filled the air in a confusing whirl. Eadha, knocked off her feet in the middle of it all, barely avoided being trampled as Tolljur rushed forward, a growl coming from his throat, and engaged the chief's son. She crawled out of the way, taking poor Aileen with her, the other girl sobbing in fright.

"What is happening?" Aileen wailed.

Not sure, Eadha gave no answer. The circle of onlookers widened instinctively, no one wanting to get in the way of—Tolljur, it must be Tolljur, her master. Aye indeed it was…but transformed.

He wore not the great bearskin that usually served to identify him but only a simple woolen tunic over his leather trews, with his golden-brown hair hanging loose around his shoulders. That did not make him any less terrifying.

She put her arms around Aileen, gritted her teeth and began to pray.

Lugh, Lugh...

Och, she knew not for what to ask. This that she beheld must be the berserker's rage such as she'd glimpsed during the attack back home. And it seemed beyond all reach of prayer.

Like an animal and not a man, Tolljur attacked the chief's son, who went unarmed save for his fists. Those he had already used on Aileen, as witnessed by the purple bruise rising livid on her pale face.

One of Friti's cronies tossed him a knife even as Tolljur, glittering blade raised, flew in upon him. But Friti had little chance against such frenzy—no man had.

Screams erupted even as the knives met in desperate, tight, and crashing blows. Friti, immediately at a disadvantage, turned several of these before falling back into the crowd. Tolljur, an indescribable rictus of fury on his face, followed, and everyone began hollering at once.

Eadha, with Aileen clutched in her arms, could only stare in mingled horror and fascination. She would not mind watching Friti die, for she could see—and more importantly feel—what he was, an animal far worse than any bear. And part of her thrilled to Tolljur's anger that echoed her own, even as his transformation terrified her.

Then, uncannily, time seemed to slow down. She saw everything in exaggerated motion; the great, swinging swipes of Tolljur's knife, the appearance of the chief, Gunnar, running in with another man, who wore a cloak of black feathers. She saw the chief and

Friti's cronies fall upon Tolljur even as his blade reached for Friti's throat, only to be thrown off again and again, his great berserker strength making nothing of their combined efforts.

Bright red blood sprang from Friti's chest, and he fell to the ground, shattering a water vessel. A crowd of men, bellowing, fell again on Tolljur and—most incredible of all—a door suddenly opened in Eadha's mind.

And she could sense him, he who had shielded himself against her ability until now. Abruptly she found herself inside his mind seeing, feeling, and raging.

She experienced his overwhelming fury and the accompanying rush of strength, like a wave that tore at him even as it triumphed. She felt the darkness, the fire and pain, pain, *pain.*

Totally engaged, as caught as he, she flailed when hard hands caught at him and hauled him back, the fury responding with increased vigor. She felt the magic settle on him like a weight as the man in the raven-feather cloak raised his hands and cast what could only be a spell.

The berserker rage abated—not much, but enough to allow the men present to subdue Tolljur. Only then did the chief, Gunnar, bellow, "You have slain my son! The penalty for that is death."

With her divided awareness—part of it still belonging to her and part trapped within Tolljur's equally trapped mind—Eadha found it hard to comprehend. She looked at Friti in mingled victorious fury and trepidation, and saw that, aye, he appeared dead. Then she became distracted by the fact that she could understand what Gunnar had said.

Even though he spoke in his own tongue.

She listened through Tolljur's ears. Felt his agony and distress. Remained at one with him.

The shock of it held her pinned even as the man in the raven-feather cloak spoke. "He is not dead. And a man in the throes of berserker rage is not responsible for his actions."

Awareness began trickling back to Tolljur—Eadha felt it come like sand through clenched fingers. With it came his control, like iron, that until now had successfully kept her out. It turned her connection to him fragile and brittle, chased her from him until the bright sunlight danced in dots before her eyes and she could no longer feel Aileen's fingers clutching at her.

What happened? Tolljur asked before she slipped from his mind.

The man in the raven cloak shouted in a rough voice—Eadha could no longer understand him. She saw him come to Tolljur's defense, much as she had come to Aileen's, saw the stoic expression return to Tolljur's face.

But she had already experienced his confusion and pain, had felt it all.

Her empathy had not failed her; his strength had merely held her at bay.

Now time snapped back into place and sped impossibly. Too many voices hollered, too many emotions bombarded her. She dragged Aileen to her feet even as others helped Friti up.

No, he was not dead. Curse it! But bright blood colored his face and the front of his rent tunic, and more of the same streaked Tolljur's arms. Had Friti marked him? While in his mind, Eadha had felt no hint of pain.

Gunnar barked questions and gave orders, none of which Eadha could understand. Friti's companions answered him; Tolljur, the knife still dangling from his fingers, said nothing.

Suddenly Eadha found Inger at her side. The woman spoke in Eadha's ear. "Go to your master."

"Eh?" Eadha, still uncomprehending, gazed into Inger's eyes. "But he will not want me near him. And I need to take Aileen—"

"You will do as you are told." Inger's lips twisted. "I saw what happened, and I will take the girl home. Kaddi will lead your master home with him. You go along."

"I do no' understand."

But Eadha remembered what lay inside Tolljur, the gulf of bewilderment and want. Aye, he would need her.

Shrugging off all hesitation, she released Aileen to Inger's care and stepped forward to Tolljur's side.

Chapter Nine

Kaddi's hut, far up the rocky slope, seemed dim inside after the bright sunlight, even though a fire burned at the center of the floor. Smoke trailed up and through the air to compete with the single beam of radiance filtering down through the roof vent, and Eadha's throat immediately closed.

At the rough direction of the man in the raven-feather cloak, she'd positioned herself beneath Tolljur's shoulder in order to keep him upright while they climbed. The task grew easier as they went and Tolljur's strength returned. She could feel his heart beating against her breast. She could smell him, the tang of his sweat and a coppery hint of blood.

And, barely more than a whisper, she could yet feel him, as if the merest remnants of their connection remained. He had, aye, slammed the door, seeking to defend himself. But it had not shut completely enough.

Against her will, her sympathies stirred and her heart softened. She had sensed much from these Norse men since being captured. Nothing like what lay within Tolljur.

"Ease him down." The old man in the raven-feather cloak—Kaddi—spoke to her in a rough appropriation of her own tongue. She lowered Tolljur beside the hearth, and Kaddi kicked the door shut. No one had followed them from the lower part of the settlement.

Now the smoky air gathered around them, closing them in.

She looked at Tolljur, who stared straight ahead from empty eyes. Emotions she did not understand caught at her, and in a whisper she asked, "Is he all right?"

Kaddi gave her a glare from his one eye—the right. The absence of the other left a puckered socket that gave him a permanent squint. Silver hair sprouted from his head and chin, tumbling over his chest in a wild beard. Emanating from him…

Power. She remembered the magic he'd cast below, that seemed to interrupt Tolljur's fury. Eadha had felt that kind of power before, back home, from Neal—the old druid priest.

Aye, she recognized this.

Kaddi's remaining eye, faded blue, inspected her. "To be sure, he is far from right. You understand nothing."

Eadha bit at her lip. Suddenly she wanted to understand, forgetting for the first time her own predicament.

Kaddi began to bustle about, fetching a basin of water and bandaging. These he thrust at Eadha. "Here, girl, do something useful. You are supposed to be his servant, *nei*?"

"Aye." She accepted the basin. "But I am not good for much."

"Ha! Honest, at least. He needs a draught, and I must prepare it. What happened back there?"

"I went to fetch water." It had seemed simple enough. Now the vessel she'd taken lay shattered and her world further shaken from its course.

"The chief's son came by with a number of companions. He wanted one of the girls there—*wanted* her, if you understand what I mean."

Kaddi snorted. "I do." He shot Eadha another hard look. "Wanted her and not you? Then how did Tolljur become involved?"

"Aileen—the lass upon whom Friti centered his attentions—she came here with me from home, captive. And the chief's son kept his eye on me the whole time he tormented her, as if baiting me. She's a member of my clan, see—I think she was claimed by another that night."

"That is 'Master' Friti to you, even if he does behave like a rutting boar. As son of the jarl, he feels he has a right to any woman here if the fancy takes him. And it usually does take him—even if she's another man's slave."

"Truly?" Eadha stared, appalled.

"And some not slaves. What did you do?"

"I—I spoke up in her defense."

"As Friti knew you would. He did not bait you so much as your master—the fool. The quarrel between those two is an old one. Well—sponge the blood from him, girl. Why do you just stand there?"

Eadha dropped to her knees at Tolljur's side and set the basin down carefully. Tolljur did not so much as look at her. She could feel less and less from him now.

What went on in his mind? Within his spirit?

She wrung out the cloth that floated in the basin and inspected the work to be done.

Blood trickled down both Tolljur's arms. Aye, Friti had touched him, and more than once. Gently she began to wipe the blood from the first cut, and the last of the connection between them broke.

Did that mean he had increased the hard control he kept on himself? An effort, was it, to remain stoical against the pain? Well, she supposed he would need such a defense.

A shadow moved through the smoke, and Kaddi leaned in above her. "How bad is it? Ah, *ja*—those cuts are not deep. Not like the others he bears."

"Others?"

Kaddi bent a fierce look on her. "So—you have not seen your master without his clothing. That answers one question. He did not come through that last raid unscathed. The bear is a hard master."

"I see." Eadha peered into Tolljur's face. Where had he gone? The still-empty eyes argued he had retreated far. Carefully she finished cleaning one arm, her fingers brushing warm skin over tight muscle, and moved to the other.

Kaddi snorted in approval. "You may not be good at much, as you say, but I like the way you tend him. Gentle. He needs that."

To her own surprise, Eadha began to relax. This odd old man proved the first she'd encountered here with whom she did not feel uncomfortable. Indeed, being in his presence felt familiar, akin to being with old Neal back home.

The feeling loosened her tongue. She asked, "Is he always like this when he comes out of a fit?"

"*Ja.* But he has not come out as yet. In battle, you understand, the bear's rage would go on and on, taking its toll on the body of the man. There, bandage those cuts. Your fingers are not so rough as mine."

"Can he hear us? What we are saying, I mean."

"*Ja*. He will come out of it soon. Give him this."

He passed Eadha a wooden cup, the contents of which gave off a powerful woodsy scent.

She balked. "What is it?"

Kaddi snapped, "It is not your place to ask. Would you question those who know far more than you?"

Eadha answered instinctively as she might Neal, "Questioning is the best way to learn."

"Ah." Kaddi began to laugh, a sharp cackle. "Our bear has a rare find here. Perhaps a treasure in disguise, *nei*?"

Eadha peered into the cup. "What will this do to him?"

"For—*for* him, girl. That drink will impart strength and help to clear his mind. It is but a mild dose. Trust me."

Eadha had no choice. She tipped the cup to Tolljur's lips, leaning up on her knees and very nearly into his arms. His scent rushed over her again, competing with that of the potion.

"How long will it take to work?"

Kaddi cackled again. "Watch and see."

The dose duly given, Eadha returned to her bandaging. Kaddi moved around the hut behind her, somewhere in the smoke, and time trickled by like water from a leaking vessel. She looked up from tying the last bandage to find Tolljur's gaze resting on her, clear and aware.

Breath she did not remember holding gusted from her lungs. "Och! Are you better now?"

He did not reply. The clear, silvery eyes moved from her to the old man, who came bustling up and spoke into Tolljur's face.

"Fool! Why would you rise to Friti's bait? It is a good thing you did not kill him."

Tolljur blinked but did not speak. Eadha rushed into his silence.

"You are wrong," she told Kaddi. "It seems a fine thing to me, were that one removed from the world."

"*Ja*, and so it might well be. But he is the jarl's son, and Gunnar is not the man to make allowances when it comes to those of his blood. The very least that would happen is this one here," he jerked his head at Tolljur, "would be banished."

"So? Again—not a terrible thing."

"Again," Kaddi returned swiftly, "you know nothing. Our people have already been banished from home. It is why we settled here in this land of ice and steam."

"Why?" Eadha asked. "Why were they banished?"

"Gunnar, as a young man, offended his king. He was not so different from Friti then and wished to take his pleasure where he would. He chose the wrong woman."

Eadha nodded.

Kaddi went on, "My point is, should *he* be banished," he once more jerked his head at Tolljur, "there would be nowhere in this wide world for him to go."

"I see."

"Do you?" Kaddi's faded blue eye narrowed. "He came to your defense, *ja*? It could have cost him dear. Your duty is to keep that from happening again." The old man smiled, revealing filed teeth. "I sense much in you, girl. I sense that you may feel much."

Eadha's eyes widened.

"Use that ability wisely."

"Eadha, you are unhurt?" The deeper voice interrupted their conversation. She turned her head and found Tolljur's gaze fixed on her, clarity in his pale eyes.

She grimaced. The roots of her hair hurt, and she would be black and blue all down one side where Friti had thrown her to the ground. But something kept her from admitting that to this man whose vulnerability she had now tasted.

"Well enough," she replied. "But you…"

He stirred, straightened his back, and stretched his arms, scrutinizing them with mild surprise. He lifted his gaze to Kaddi.

"What happened?" he spoke still in Eadha's tongue.

"What do you remember?"

Tolljur shook his head, his gaze returning to Eadha. "Friti."

"*Ja*, that says it all. Sit quietly. Rest."

The old man once more bustled away.

Feeling awkward, Eadha gestured at the cup. "Master Kaddi made that for you; you had best finish it."

"Master Kaddi, is it?" Tolljur's bisected eyebrow lifted. "You, paying such respect?"

"Does he not deserve it?"

"*Ja*."

Silence fell between them, during which Tolljur drained the cup. He lowered it and bent a look upon Eadha. "What did happen back there? Tell me all of it."

"I went to fetch water. I fear your water vessel is now smashed."

"I care nothing for that."

"Many others were at the pool when I arrived. One among them was a lass brought away from home—my home—called Aileen. I know not who claimed her."

Tolljur shrugged.

"I was glad—relieved—to see her. We exchanged words. Then the chief's son came with some fellows. He looked at me but spoke to Aileen, first in his tongue so we could not understand, then in ours. He demanded—"

"You do not need to say."

Impulsively, Eadha leaned closer to Tolljur. Would he understand? "She was so afraid. Terrified, and still shattered by being taken by a stranger—treated as you have no' treated me." Eadha stated it plainly. "Raped."

Emotion flickered in Tolljur's eyes, but he did not speak.

"I had to take her part. I had to!"

Slowly and with regret he shook his head. "You did not have to. You should have kept your eyes down, minded your own path."

Passionately she said, "I am no' made that way. Anyhow, given who I am, she looks to me—"

Abruptly she broke off. She had almost given herself away as the chief's daughter.

Tolljur tipped his head, and the straight, golden brown hair slid over one shoulder. "You must guard yourself against Friti as against a wild beast. He did not truly want your friend. He wanted to stir you—and through you, me."

"I understand that now."

"He knew I would seek to protect you. As for your friend—he will have her anyway if he chooses. Only

73

her master can hope to protect her, and not many are willing to step forward against Friti."

"Except you." For some reason Eadha's heart started to pound. Fearless he was, and strong.

He set his cup on the floor beside the hearth. Almost casually he said, "So now you have beheld the berserker's rage. Yet you do not shy from me in terror."

A tangle of emotions sprang up in Eadha's breast: a measure of wariness there remained, and caution. Surprising protectiveness, allegiance, and something else she had no ability to name.

Still kneeling at his knee, she gazed into his eyes and said, "Nay, Master Tolljur—I will not turn away."

Chapter Ten

Tolljur dreamed of fire and awoke to pain. He lay in the near dark with his heart hammering and the breath coming fast in his lungs, trying to reassert the control that had fled him in sleep.

For several terrifying moments it refused to come. He blinked his eyes rapidly in the dim room and wondered why.

The loss of control—of his self—beset him whenever he was overtaken by the bear. He kept it fiercely in place at all other times when he faced adversity, uncertainty, passion or pain. But the dream of burning and loss had overset him. And memory even now battered at him. He had seen his sister in the dream; she had called to him for help, for saving.

He had failed her—once again.

For several terrible moments, lying with his chest heaving, he could not tell physical pain from the other kind. He sought to master both and did not succeed.

He listened to Eadha's breathing from the other side of the hut, and the sound brought some comfort. Three days had passed since his confrontation with Friti at the pool. In the hall last night, where Tolljur had gone alone, Gunnar had spoken of another voyage soon, asking whether his warriors were ready.

Tolljur, of course, had not demurred. The chief had no idea how badly injured he was—no one knew, save

Kaddi. Not even Eadha.

The stubborn wound high up on his right shoulder, inflicted by one of Eadha's clansmen in the attack that had seen her captured, refused to heal. He knew wounds, especially those to his own flesh, and suspected this one must have poisoned.

He should go to Kaddi, rouse the old man from his bed, and seek treatment. But at this moment, staring into the gloom, he feared he had not the strength to rise.

He cursed softly. Lack of strength equaled lack of control, and that he could not allow.

He sat up with a groan, and the hazy half-light danced around him. Moonlight filtered down through the smoke hole. His new slave had let the fire go out again.

He had to admit Eadha proved woefully inept at many things. She neglected the fire, burned his food, and could not sweep dust out the door. She spoke when she should keep silent and, when they went forth, refused to lower her eyes.

Yet he found some ease in her presence. He enjoyed looking at her, letting his gaze slide along the length of her hair, and seeking to decipher the fleeting moods that crossed her face. Oddly, the more he looked the more her slightly angled, freckled countenance became lovely to him despite the mark on her cheek. Or perhaps even because of it...

He would not care to lose her now.

Another involuntary groan tore from him as he strove—unsuccessfully—to rise from his bed.

"What is it, Tolljur?"

The soft query floated to him across the hut. When had Eadha awakened? He compressed his lips. She should call him Master Tolljur, but in that battle he did not care to engage.

"Return to sleep," he told her shortly.

Of course she did not obey. He heard her rise, and a moment later caught the soft patter of her bare feet as she crossed the room to his bed. Then the scent of her enfolded him as she bent near, that of her hair and body warmed by sleep.

She touched him carefully, a hand on his brow. He liked the way Eadha touched him, not as if she felt fear and with none of Anaborg's greed.

"You are ill. Burning with fever."

"I fear one of my wounds has poisoned, despite all Kaddi's efforts."

"Let me see. We need some light."

She hurried to strike a rush light, using flint since the fire lay dead. He sat where he was, heart pounding. He did not want to see what lay beneath his tunic.

"Go get Kaddi," he bade her. "Have him bring me one of his draughts."

She snorted. "I do not doubt those draughts of his are half the trouble. What is in them, do you ken?"

"What I need."

"So—he doses you." In the new-flared light she regarded him steadily.

He shrugged painfully. "Lesser of evils."

Breath grated from between her lips. "Let's get this off you and see."

It took both of them to wrestle the soft sleeping tunic over his head, and by the time it came off he sweated in agony.

Eadha gasped. The big, ragged wound at his shoulder looked puffy and enflamed. Streaks of red radiated from it down his chest and arm.

"You are right; this is poisoned. Something must be done."

"Go fetch Kaddi," he repeated.

"Aye, perhaps. This is beyond any skill I possess."

"Are you a healer?" He squinted up at her through the waves of pain.

"Nay."

"I suppose you have tended your husband."

She stiffened, and he rued reminding her of her loss.

Yet he persisted, "Was he killed in the attack?" Perhaps better if he had been; then she need not long to return to him. Though why he, Tolljur, should care how she longed for some distant husband, he could not say. And of course, grief might be as hard to master as longing.

She did not answer his question. "I will run and fetch Kaddi. You lie quietly while I am gone."

The place seemed twice as quiet after she went. She left the door standing open, and faint moonlight spilled in to dance through the air.

Tolljur wondered if he were dying. Death in battle might be hard to come by for one such as he, but the madness made no proof against illness.

Wracked by pain, he sat staring out the door and thought about the possibility of death. Had he earned a place in Valhalla? Death in battle would assure it. Anyway, he found he cared less about himself than what might happen to Eadha should this fever burn him to cinders. He had no family to take over his property. Gunnar would claim her, and before his funeral flames died she would be in Friti's hands.

He emitted another groan, this one not earned by any physical wound.

****

"Hurry—faster. He is in a terrible bad way."

The old man stumped behind Eadha, negotiating the slope far too slowly for her liking. The combination of summer's gloaming and moonlight afforded sufficient light by which to see, and she had burdened herself with all the things he insisted on bringing. Why could he not pick up the pace?

Kaddi grunted. "Is that any way to speak to me, girl? Where is your respect?"

"I left it behind at the hut. Did you not bid me look after him? So I am doing."

"Then give me your arm. I am not so young as I was."

In his haste, Kaddi had neglected to don his raven-feather cloak; he looked aged and felt frail when he seized Eadha's arm in fingers like talons. He leaned on her heavily.

Eadha sought to temper her impatience. Why did she care so about a member of these vile marauders, the very same who had killed her people and dragged her from her home?

Yet care about Tolljur she did, and she was near as breathless as Kaddi when they made it down the slope to the dwelling. She had seen folk—her own folk—sick with fever. The outcome had rarely proved good.

"Stir up the fire," Kaddi told her as he limped in. "And shut the door. What we do here is not for prying eyes."

But Eadha went instead to Tolljur. He lay on his bed, tossing fitfully, his eyes glassy. "I am returned," she told him. "I ha' brought Kaddi."

His only response came in a low groan. Kaddi stumped up and bent over him, elbowing Eadha aside.

"Get me more light," he commanded. "And let me look at him."

Eadha obeyed, listening as Kaddi began a low conversation with his patient. Unable to understand what they said, Eadha felt her frustration rise again. Tolljur responded in answers of only one or two words, too sore hurt to offer more. The old man clicked his tongue and laid a horny hand on Tolljur's brow, turning to Eadha at last.

"The fool has stripped away the bandaging. No wonder the wound poisoned."

"How bad is it?"

"Bad."

"Surely not mortal?"

Kaddi gave her a sharp look out of his remaining eye. "Do you care?"

Eadha's stomach tightened, and she fought an inner battle. "Aye."

"Good. He needs someone to care about him. Else he does foolish things like shedding his bandages and taking sore risks."

Tolljur's voice issued from the bed—a single word that sounded like a protest.

Kaddi turned on him. "It is true. And she will need to take care of you, if you wish to survive."

The only answer came in another groan.

Kaddi seized Eadha's arm again. "List to me, girl. If he goes out of his head with fever, the madness may well lay claim to him, and that will drain his strength. You must keep him calm, at all cost, until the fever breaks."

"Are you certain it will break?"

"I will do all in my power to assure so. But meanwhile, if you have any prayers, speak them."

Pray? For one of her conquerors? Eadha balked. She might not wish Tolljur dead. But approaching the beautiful and sacred on his behalf defied contemplation.

In order to quiet the old man, she nodded and bade him curtly, "Do your work."

****

Dawn arrived unnoticed as Eadha tended the fire, fetched and carried, and answered Kaddi's every demand. Long before the settlement stirred, Tolljur lapsed into unconsciousness, still tossing on his bed and muttering in his own tongue.

Eadha watched with trepidation as Kaddi pondered the angry wound—just one of several that marked Tolljur beneath his clothing—and brewed not one but two potions, each of which he tipped to Tolljur's lips.

Barely responsive, Tolljur choked on them and grunted in protest.

"What is that you are giving him?" Eadha demanded as she might of Neal, back home.

Kaddi shot her another sharp glare. "Can you not trust me, girl? He does."

Unsatisfied, Eadha returned, "No reason not to tell me what you ha' put in there."

"The first is to purify his blood. The second to calm him and fight the onset of madness."

"Oh."

"You will need to guard him well this day, turn everyone from the door. Can you do that?"

"Aye."

81

"The fever should peak by midday. Until then, you will need to keep him calm."

"How?"

"Do whatever you must. I will help as I can."

"More potions?" Eadha's lip curled.

"A word of advice, girl—you will not survive long here if you display such disrespect. Right now he stands between you and harm. Only, you see he is no longer standing, is he? Do you have any notion what may happen to you should he die?"

Eadha thought about it and bit her lip. "Aye."

"Then mend your attitude and tend him well."

"I will. My apologies, Master Kaddi. I intended no disrespect."

"I do not know who you were in your past life, girl. Here you are a slave. Best to remember that."

Tolljur's eyelids fluttered; beneath them his eyes rolled. He muttered a word, and Eadha leaned forward.

"What did he say?"

Kaddi rose to his feet with a grunt. "Your name, girl. I believe that was your name."

Chapter Eleven

"Please be still. Please." Eadha laid both her palms on Tolljur's bare chest, nearly weeping with distress. Noon had come and gone, and Kaddi had departed without explanation. Outside Tolljur's hut, the door to which she kept tight shut, the day warmed. Inside, her new master worsened.

Now he tossed and flailed, senseless, his skin searing to her touch. So far, though, the madness had not come. Kaddi had told her what to watch for: stiffening in every limb, eyes rolling back in his head, and the strength of ten men.

Nay this was just fever, but dire enough.

She glanced toward the hearth, where stood prepared two more draughts. The old man had bidden her give them to Tolljur if the fever worsened, and without question it had. But she hated to dose Tolljur again when she could not divine the contents. They smelled sharp and deadly.

Instead she sponged him against the fever, wringing out her cloth in cool water again and again, bathing his brow and wiping down his limbs.

Already his thrashing tore the bandaging Kaddi had placed during the night. Eadha smoothed it with clumsy fingers.

He fought against her then, his strength formidable even in the absence of the madness. Should that come

83

upon him, how would she ever keep him still?

Upon the thought, Tolljur thrashed yet again, muttering words she did not understand, and reared up in the blankets. His eyes went wide, and he stared forward at nothing.

Eadha, going hot and cold with desperation, clutched at his shoulders. She would have to give him the dose after all.

"Please," she begged again. And in her head, *Please, Lugh.*

Courage, lass. Use all the strengths you have to save him.

Ah, so the voice had returned, had it? That which she'd not heard in days…

She gazed into Tolljur's eyes. Did he focus on her? For the barest instant it seemed so. But then, despite her hands on his shoulders, he reared once more and struggled to rise.

At that moment the hut door opened. Turning her head, Eadha half expected to see Inger. It had already crossed her mind to go fetch the older woman, only she dared not leave Tolljur alone.

Instead she saw the wizened form of Kaddi, his silver head bent over the object he held in his hands.

By all that was holy—it was a clairsach.

Eadha's battered mind almost failed to recognize the instrument. For, how came such a thing to this place? She stared, and Kaddi grimaced.

"I just put that vixen to the run," he greeted Eadha.

"Vixen?"

"Anaborg Helmsdottir," Kaddi answered shortly. "She was about to come pushing in here." Kaddi shot Tolljur a sharp look. "No better?"

"Worse. The fever has not yet broken. I cannot keep him still."

"This will help."

Kaddi thrust the harp at Eadha; she accepted it by reflex. A lovely object, it measured a bit smaller than hers, left back home, and had been carved in twining patterns all up and down the post.

No Norse creation, this. Stolen. Just like her.

"How did you come by this?"

"It was not easy. I had to bargain. But I am still due some respect, and succeeded, in the end."

"To whom did it belong?"

Kaddi shrugged. "Does it matter?"

It did. Such an instrument would have been dearly loved, treasured, and possibly taken from its owner by force.

"It was broken and has been repaired." Kaddi nodded at the harp. "I trust it will not affect the sound. You did say you can play. Or did Inger say? I suggest you prove it."

"Why?"

Kaddi nodded toward Tolljur. "It is one of the few things that can give him ease."

****

Fire burned Tolljur from head to toes, unrelenting. Aye, he had dreamed of flames and the cruel drive of the madness. The agony of it still seared him, and yet…

His ear caught a sound: it shivered through the flames clear as birdsong, insinuating itself into his consciousness and bringing him up from the depths.

Music.

No tune he recognized, this, but a complicated whirl of notes that twined and twisted, engaging him and drawing him from his misery. For the first time since the coming of the fever, his heartbeat calmed. Breath came easier in his lungs, and his knotted muscles relaxed.

Someone tipped a cup to his lips, but he pushed it away. He wanted only to listen.

The music spoke of the sea, of far-reaching silver-blue waters, and the promise of eternity. He stood on a rise overlooking the ocean; gazing away southward.

Toward home.

The breeze pressed against him and blew away everything but one longing: to love. To be loved. To claim a life of love, deep as the sea, for his own.

Impossible desire. And yet the music spoke to him, soothed and promised, wove a spell so pure it felt like healing.

"There, now." A voice spoke at his ear. Kaddi?

He cared not. He rode the waves of the enchanting music and prayed it would not stop.

Father Odin.

But Odin did not come to him. Instead another appeared, tall and shining in his godliness, a spear in his hand. Was it the glorious Baldur? Maybe so—for he seemed full of light.

Blessed, Tolljur tumbled into sleep, and the god, whoever he might be, answered his prayer. For the tune went on and on.

****

The magical music accompanied Tolljur through the fire and darkness that followed. No sooner would the pain rouse him from sleep than the shiver of notes would begin anew, not always the same tune, but each equally winding and intricate. The music beat back the pain and allowed him to breathe.

Then suddenly he came to himself, sweat-soaked yet clear-headed. He lay quietly, absorbing his surroundings. His own hut, *ja,* filled with the light from several fir-tips. By their radiance, an incredible sight met his eyes.

A woman sat beside his bed, clad in a plain gown. Her hair hung loose over her back and shoulders, a river of deep waves that captured the light with glints of red. Her face appeared intent and in her hands…

A harp of Alban design. His mind fished for the word: *clairsach.* The sheen of its wooden post matched the woman's hair almost exactly, and the grace of her fingers as they moved on the strings humbled him.

Did he know her? Surely, deep in his heart, he did. A bond existed between them, fragile yet founded in devotion.

A goddess, she must surely be. Freya? *Ja,* perhaps. He lay with his newly-eased breath held, afraid to disturb the spell she wove and feeling the music touch every part of his body and mind, knitting ravaged flesh and soothing stirred spirit.

The music never faltered until the woman looked up and caught his gaze on her. Then her fingers stilled on the strings, leaving only a few notes that quivered into silence like the last whispered words of an incantation.

He recognized her the instant her eyes met his. Eadha, his servant. And his heart twisted inside him, with emotions he could not name.

"Do not stop, please." But he spoke in his own tongue, and so she did not heed him. She set the instrument aside, and he could have wept in protest.

"How do you feel?" she asked and, not giving him a chance to reply, added, "I think your fever has finally broken."

"Fever?"

She laid her fingers on his brow with inexplicable familiarity, and the darkness lingering inside him ebbed a little. *Ja*, magic.

"Aye, at last," she breathed. "Thank the gods."

Was it possible she cared? His befuddled senses barely comprehended it.

"What has happened?" he asked in confusion.

She returned, "Be at peace and do not worry. You have been very ill. Do you not remember?"

"*Nei.*"

He wished she would touch him again, wanted it with an intensity that shocked him. But she rose from her rug and moved away. He heard the clack of crockery before she came back with a mug in her hands.

"Here, you need to drink this. Nay, 'tis none of the old man's vile potions, but clear, cool water."

"Kaddi?"

"He has been here caring for you—he and I." She tipped the cup to Tolljur's lips, and then, when he strove to sit up, helped him with one hand at his back. Her touch went right through him, lending strength.

He drank greedily, and she went on speaking. "I meant to go fetch Inger, if you were not better today. She has been by twice, but I did not let her in because I knew how she would fuss." She added unequivocally, "I would not let anyone in."

Tolljur gazed into her eyes and wondered what had moved her to tend him. He had no call to expect such allegiance, such—such kindness.

"How long?" he asked. "How long with fever?"

"Three days. That wound at your shoulder took poisoning." She set aside the empty cup and bent forward to peer into his face. "Why did you no' say you were hurting? And why did you remove the bandages Master Kaddi put on?"

Tolljur looked down at himself. Bare-chested, clad only in his leggings, the wounds he had taken in the raid on Eadha's settlement were now well-swaddled. How could he explain?

Stoically he said, "The wound tore during the fray with Friti, over that servant. I never went back to Kaddi with it. The old man makes a heavy-handed nurse. And I am supposed to be above pain."

"Aye, but are you?" She bent still closer and, once again, Tolljur caught her scent—clean and beguiling. A spear of desire shot through him, stealing all his sense. Suddenly he wanted to kiss her so much he could think of nothing else.

"Am I?" he repeated stupidly, his gaze on her lips. Maybe he could will it so.

"Are you above pain? I ken you are, during a fit, but you are no' in a fit now."

"I have a high threshold for pain," he admitted. But what of pleasure? He'd had few chances to put that to the test.

Anaborg kept promising to take him to the highest peaks—but he wanted no promises or anything else from her. This woman, on the other hand—she seemed as mysterious as her music, able to engage his mind as well as his body.

And what of his heart?

"Are you hungry?" she asked. "I have kept some broth warming." She wrinkled her nose. "I will warn you, I prepared it, so 'tis no' very good."

To his own surprise, Tolljur smiled. "No one can be good at everything."

"Nay, I suppose not."

"And it seems you have cared well for me, *ja*?"

"I did try. I fed you Kaddi's vile potions and sponged you against the fever."

Ach, and he had missed it. With deceptive calm he told her, "I still feel a little warm now."

"Truly? Only let me fetch the basin. I will cool you down once again."

"*Ja*." Please, Odin.

"And," he added carefully, "then you might play some more of that music."

Chapter Twelve

"He needs to get out into the air, and this house needs sweeping. I do not know what is wrong with you, girl! Why did you not call me to help tend him? I would have done a much better job than you."

Inger delivered the words with her usual stridency, a woman used to being obeyed. Tolljur, on his feet for the first time in days and feeling far less ready for it than he cared to admit, turned his gaze on Eadha, expecting contrition.

Not so. Instead, his slave toed up to Inger, nothing intimidated.

"I needed no help from you."

Inger directed a scandalized look at Tolljur. "Are you going to let her speak to me that way?"

Tolljur raised his eyebrows. Inger had left the door of the hut wide open when she barged in, and he had to admit the place did need sweeping as well as fresh rushes and some of the ash emptied out of the hearth.

His servant, in fact, made a poor servant. He cared little for that. Since he'd awakened following the fever, he'd wanted nothing but to kiss her every time he looked at her.

He could not explain it. Neither alluring nor particularly beautiful—save for her hair—she seemed to have got somehow inside him, past the defenses he kept raised so firmly.

"I am as well cared for as I could ask," he told Inger. A lie. His desire demanded more.

For an instant, he let himself think about it: Eadha hot and willing beneath him, the magic so particular to her engaging and then claiming his spirit.

Heat flooded through him, and Inger narrowed her eyes. "Fool," she spat and dismissed him from her attention.

She rounded on Eadha instead. "Do your duty by him, girl."

"So I have been."

"*Ja*? Have you learned to make bread without burning it? Grain is precious here in Husavik, I will have you know. Hard to grow and valuable as silver, in a raid. Not for wasting! Have you aired his blankets? Have you taken him to the bath house?"

"Eh?" Eadha responded. "We bathe here."

Inger rocked back on her heels. "Do you not know the difference? In the bath house he will sweat, purifying his body. No wonder these wounds took poisoning."

"Just the one of them," Eadha returned. Tolljur tried not to smile. He could not remember the last time anyone had given Inger as good as she dealt. But Eadha showed no signs of backing down.

"Take him now," Inger snapped.

"Now? He is barely on his feet."

And as a man—a berserker, no less—of nearly thirty winters, should he not be allowed to speak for himself? Yet Tolljur found he enjoyed hearing Eadha speak for him.

Inger lowered her voice a notch, indicating confidentiality. "Word has it Gunnar will send the next raiding party out within the week."

Eadha looked taken aback. "Well, he cannot go. He is not ready."

"I cannot stay behind." Tolljur stepped forward and touched Eadha's arm; fire flared where his fingers met her soft flesh. "I am—what would you call it? The head of the spear."

"Then Gunnar must be made to delay."

Inger laughed. "You do not know the man. Heedlessness is what got him here. He is not likely to change."

For once, Eadha appeared speechless. Tolljur tightened his grip on her arm. "We will go to the bath house. I will soon regain my strength, as you will see."

Inger nodded decisively. "The two of you go—and you teach her where her duties lie, Tolljur. I shall stay and clean this place properly while you are out of the way."

Duly chased, Tolljur and Eadha stepped out into the bright sunlight, where Tolljur's eyes instinctively marked all the things he loved about Husavik: the deep blue sky reflected in the still deeper blue waters of the bay, the green and gray slope of the land, and the gulls soaring overhead.

He had been born in another place, *ja*, where lay a deep fjord and rocky cliffs, but he had come here with his family and a large company of Norse settlers when but eight. As Gunnar's berserker, his father had a place of honor but had never been close to the chief in friendship. They had disagreed on far too many things. But Magnus Bearshirt had thrown his lot in with the young man who declared himself jarl—at that time outcast by his king—and come to settle in this new land.

For a time, life had been good. Tolljur remembered running and playing with his sister and the other youngsters of the settlement. He remembered his father training him at arms, as well as seeking to prepare him for the life of a berserker.

Never show weakness, even if you feel it.

Things had changed after his father, and then his mother, died. Gunnar had come into his own by then, and his son, Friti, grew into the bully he was still. And Tolljur, left to defend his sister, had failed.

He drew a breath, and Eadha shot him a close look. "Are you sure you are up to this?"

"*Ja.* Come."

She removed her bare arm from under his fingers, but only so she could tuck it beneath his elbow more securely, supporting him. "Where is this bath house?"

"To the right, near the harbor. I will show you."

They went slowly, and people stared. Some greeted Tolljur in passing. Others merely gave Eadha disapproving stares. She was meant to follow behind her master respectfully, should they venture out together. Not accompany him holding his arm proprietorially, like a wife.

That thought, appearing seemingly from the remnants of the fever, promptly took possession of Tolljur's mind. *Eadha, his wife.* Some men, not already wed, did marry their slaves, but it happened seldom enough. Female slaves existed for using, not cherishing.

Yet with her as his wife, he would have greater power to protect her. And if he wed her, would that not assure she must stay with him?

A shiver pierced his body at the thought, and she

gave him another doubtful look. "I still think this a bad idea. Is this bath house not a public place?"

"*Ja*."

"And will you be expected to strip down at least partly?"

"Those there go naked, *ja*." Though he hoped at this time of day the bath house might prove empty.

"Then everyone will see your bandages. I thought you did not wish folk to know you are injured."

"I am known to carry wounds—always. I cannot be seen defeated by them."

"I assume that is some form of male pride?"

"Far more than that." He wondered if, coming from her world, she could ever understand. "I am berserker. Undefeatable—at least, in battle."

She thought about that for several moments, her expression one of consternation. "But—did your father not die?"

"*Ja*, clubbed down during the fight and then trampled by a score of men. He did not die then but was carried home and only perished after."

He thought about the deep horror of that, seeing his father—skull crushed, face frozen in the rictus of the madness, body broken. He remembered how his mother had wept and the realization that had come to Tolljur—this would be his own fate.

It had not mattered so much these last years since Gyda's death. He had begun to look on his ultimate demise as a just and welcome release. But if something befell him now, he must fear for Eadha. He needed to protect her.

To his dismay, they found the bath house occupied after all, when they reached it. He almost turned away before two warriors, loitering outside, greeted him. Their attitudes of careful respect did not keep them from eyeing Eadha closely.

"Good morning to you, Tolljur," said the first, called Nels. "Everyone has been wondering where you were. Occupied with your new bed slave, so Friti said."

Tolljur shot Eadha a look, glad she could not understand. Gently he disengaged from her arm and pushed her behind him.

"Go you back to the hut and wait for me."

Predictably, she argued it. "But will you not need help getting back home? I will wait here."

"Just do as I ask."

Too late. Among the voices coming from inside he heard one raised—Friti numbered one of the men in the bath house. Tolljur's lips tightened.

"Go," he bade Eadha once more, but, stubborn, she stood where she was.

Friti appeared in the doorway stark naked and with every contour covered in sweat, gleaming. His sharp gaze leapt first at Tolljur and then at Eadha, like a hawk on a lemming.

"Ah, master berserker, will you not come in? And bring your new slave. There are those here who need servicing."

"I will go home," Eadha decided, taut as a bowstring.

Friti's lips stretched in a predatory smile. "*Nei,* Tolljur, bring her in. You have been keeping her too much to yourself. She needs to learn how we share."

Tolljur's heart sank. This situation could not possibly end well.

****

The hut, built from sod and wood, measured perhaps thirty by thirty paces and seemed overfilled with both steam and men. Once the skin door closed behind Eadha she could see little enough and blinked fiercely. What she could see raised the heat to her cheeks. Every warrior there, to the last man, had stripped naked.

Ah, and she did not know where to look. In the past she had seen warriors of her clan partially unclad, and this company would suppose she'd seen her mythical husband naked. Several shocked glances told her these men, no doubt the elite among their warrior kind, were big in every sense of the word, confident and intimidating.

It did not help that their emotions rushed upon her as well as their gazes: a mix of arrogance, casual cruelty, and incipient amusement. Och, and lust. As usual, she sensed little from the man beside her; he had once more shut down tightly.

But, just as if he too could sense the feelings running rife in the hut, he reached out to catch her arm and once more pushed her gently behind him.

"Go," he said softly in Eadha's tongue, and she turned to leave, in this instance wholly obedient.

"*Nei*," Friti said again and raised a commanding arm. "She will stay to serve you. And us." He also spoke in Eadha's tongue and bared his teeth in a smile before waving a hand down his naked body suggestively. "You will share, Tolljur, *ja*? As you know, slaves are fair game, and she might as well learn her duties."

He bent a bright gaze on Eadha. "Strip off, girl. Let us see what we have."

"*Nei.*" Tolljur spoke instantly. His fingers, still on Eadha's arm, felt like iron bands. She struggled to number the men in the hut through the gloom. Six. Six of them, along with one female slave, who stood with downcast eyes and wore nothing but a dampened shift and a defeated air. Eadha needed to get out of here, and quickly. If Tolljur sought to defend her—if he went berserk—he would pay for it physically in a cost she did not want to contemplate.

No sooner had the realization hit her than the skin door flew open again. Anaborg Helmsdottir stood there, barefooted and with her bright, golden hair tumbling loose down her back.

She said something in her tongue, and the assembled men, all but Tolljur, cheered.

The young female slave immediately slunk back into a corner. With a lascivious smile, Anaborg entered and immediately began to strip, rendering Eadha breathless with distress. Did the woman mean to bathe with these men? Was such a thing done in this society, and the woman not a slave?

The men hooted in appreciation as Anaborg removed her clothing. She had a well-fleshed, shapely body with full, pendulant breasts, flaring hips, and a flat stomach. As soon as the last of her garments hit the floor, one of the men called to her.

She raised a finger and, totally shameless, smiled. With a word that sounded like a promise, she turned to Tolljur.

Her wicked, blue eyes engaged his, and she spoke to him seductively as she reached for the hem of his tunic. With another wave of shock, Eadha realized Anaborg meant to divest him of his clothes.

Of course. No one went clad here. Even the downtrodden slave boasted little to cover her.

Tolljur stiffened and stood like a rock when Anaborg laid hold of him. Eadha wished desperately she could divine his emotions. She certainly felt Anaborg's, and they drenched her with embarrassed heat.

Anaborg meant to have him here and now—right in front of Eadha and all this company.

Chapter Thirteen

The men filling the bath house, with Friti at their head, all grinned as Anaborg drew the tunic over Tolljur's head, revealing his bandaged wounds. Ignoring the injuries, the woman immediately reached for the laces at the front of Tolljur's leggings, her fingers untying them with swift agility.

Eadha knew she should obey Tolljur and flee while she had the opportunity, but shock kept her rooted where she stood at his back. Would even Anaborg perform a sex act before so many eyes? Did she expect Tolljur to allow it? And what did Anaborg seek to prove? That she could pleasure any man she wished anywhere she chose, that, to her, coupling meant nothing more than a tantalizing show?

Tolljur's bare torso, half turned to Eadha, already gleamed with sweat. The hut, close and stuffy, made it hard to breathe. Eadha wondered what would happen if she passed out, and then forgot all about her own discomfort as Anaborg thrust both hands inside Tolljur's leggings.

The men all hooted again. They watched the little pageant avidly—all but Friti whose eyes now turned to Eadha instead.

He spoke, the words a taunt, and Eadha felt his lust—his cruelty—reach for her. She understood then. Once Tolljur succumbed to Anaborg, Friti would take her, Eadha, and use her as he desired.

She shrank back toward the door as protest filled her. Aye, she might turn to Tolljur for rescue, but she alone knew how weak he truly was. Och, and she should have obeyed him and run when she had the chance.

The thought no sooner penetrated her mind than Tolljur moved with abrupt speed. Anaborg, who faced Eadha, tensed, and Eadha felt her consternation.

Tolljur grunted something, and anger joined the other emotions filling Anaborg. Eadha drew a breath. If Tolljur controlled his rage, they just might get away out of this.

But Friti, still with the faint remnants of the last wounds Tolljur had inflicted visible upon him, stepped forward, grasped Eadha's wrist, and drew her to his side. In Eadha's tongue he said, "You, Tolljur, give Anaborg her heart's desire before she pleasures the rest of us. I will occupy myself with your slave—share and share alike."

Pinioned like a fish in the talons of a sea hawk, Eadha saw Tolljur turn, his silver eyes blazing with sudden wrath. Abruptly his emotions once more broke over her—sharp and raw and so dangerous they clenched her heart in an iron fist. Dread beyond what she felt of Friti exploded inside.

"Nay," she cried involuntarily.

Both men looked at her, as did Anaborg. Eadha had one glimpse of the avid cruelty in Friti's face and the hatred in Anaborg's before Tolljur's emotions overwhelmed her like a wall of fire.

Dismissing Friti, Anaborg, and even the hooting witnesses, she gazed into Tolljur's eyes. No longer clear as water, they held a storm so intense she wanted to flinch from it. She could not; these folk meant him no good. They must see the wounds upon him, yet they remained eager to watch him destroy himself.

No one but she, Eadha, could save him.

From where that thought came, she could not tell. Her emotions tangled impossibly between compassion and fear. How dared she feel protective toward this man who had taken part in the destruction of all she loved? But aye, she did feel protective toward him. She also felt for him a measure of liking and, quite inexplicably, loyalty.

All these made her lay hold of his forearms and beg him, "Nay, please. They are no' worth it."

"Listen to your slave and let us try her," Friti put in. "As your future jarl, I will have her anyway."

Already on the brink of madness, Tolljur roared, "You shall not touch her!"

His muscles, hard as wood beneath Eadha's fingers, tensed further. He brushed both her and Anaborg aside as he flew at Friti.

"Nay!" Following instinct now—far stronger than her own will—Eadha leaped for him even as he fell on the bigger man. Eadha felt the last threads of his reason stretch and fray. Everyone in the hut leaped to his feet, and the slave screamed.

Tolljur, Tolljur, please heed me. She spoke not into his ear, as she wove protective arms about him from behind, but into his mind, pushing her way past the crumbled barriers even as the madness destroyed his control, to recapture his reason.

Heed me. Do not kill him.

He gasped as Friti fell back from his rage. The face

of the jarl's son had twisted hideously into a rictus of combined hatred and caution. Being Friti, he could not keep from taunting Tolljur further.

"Go ahead—kill me," he sneered. "My father will see you spread-eagled on the stone and offered to Odin."

With a further shock, Eadha realized Friti now spoke in his own tongue; she could once more understand it through the medium of Tolljur's mind. She piggybacked his consciousness via her empathy.

Please, she whispered to him. *Please. I need you to calm.*

He drew another deep, ragged breath. She felt his emotions ease a hair as he exerted control and quite deliberately thrust her from his mind.

Friti, taking advantage, straightened and shoved Tolljur back. He did not fall, but Eadha, still clutching at him, tumbled hard to the floor.

Tolljur, the confusion clearing rapidly from his mind, spun to her. Friti got there first and hauled her up with a strong hand.

"This is not over, wench," he hissed for her ears alone. "Be certain I will have you yet."

****

Tolljur's vision cleared slowly as he and Eadha walked back to his hut, with folks staring. Outside the bath house she had tied up his leggings as a mother might those of her child.

Now, inexplicably, tears trickled down her cheeks—this woman he had not previously seen weep—and she could not seem to stop talking.

"Are you hurt? Your wound has torn open—I knew it would. 'Tis what I feared all the while. So much work

Laura Strickland

to get you through the fever, and you toss it all away on a piece of shite like that bully."

"Hush," Tolljur managed.

"Aye, I suppose I should not speak of him so, not aloud anyway. My place here has been bourn upon me, right enough. I am willing to respect my betters if I can find them. I am even prepared to respect Kaddi and possibly Inger and you…"

Tolljur's brows twitched. "I am honored."

"I refuse to respect the likes of him. Do you know what goes on in that place? Bath house, indeed."

And, Tolljur thought ruefully, what did one do with an indignant slave who felt herself his equal? His heart and mind both answered: protect her.

As she had sought to protect him. He could not deny that had happened; she had got between him and his desire to kill—or at least maim—Friti.

And for the first time in ready memory, due to her intervention, he had successfully beaten back the madness and re-exerted control.

They reached the doorway of his dwelling. He drew Eadha to a halt and turned her to face him, interrupting still another flood of words. Very gently he cupped her face in his hands and brushed away the tears with his thumbs.

Her face had gone pale, and her queer, speckled hazel eyes—bright with unshed moisture—lifted to his. She paused in mid-spate, the indignation draining from her visibly.

Something arose in Tolljur's heart, need as powerful as the rage that so often beset him. "Listen," he said. "Back there, when you got between me and Friti…you could have been hurt."

"As could you." Her gaze left his and probed the wound at his shoulder.

"Never get between a berserker and his target."

"Be that as it may, you did calm."

He struggled to express the miracle of that, this thing even he did not quite understand. "I heard your voice—in my mind. How is that possible?"

Her eyes returned to his. "I do no' ken."

"Was it magic that let you reach inside me that way?" Once the madness came upon him, nothing could stop it. Yet she had brought him back to himself. She must indeed possess some powerful magic. His eyes narrowed. "Who were you back at your home place? A druidess?"

A wary expression invaded her eyes. "Why do you ask that?"

"There was enchantment in what you did today, and there is magic in the music you play."

She pressed her lips together, and he could feel her hesitance, her reluctance to confide in him. His heart slammed in his chest; he wanted to tell her she need never fear him, that he would die before letting any harm befall her.

They stood out in the sunlight, however, with people staring.

"Come inside," he bade her instead.

They passed into the gloom of the hut, and Tolljur tied the door shut with his own hands. Once more he contemplated the morass of feelings inside. During those few moments in the bath house, everything had changed.

Slowly, he turned to face Eadha. Head lifted, she met his gaze and said, "Does it matter who I was back home? As everyone keeps telling me, that life is gone. Here—I am nothing more than a slave. Here, I belong to you."

What did he see in her eyes? Courage. Defiance. Desire? Surely not. She could not possibly want him—as he wanted her. *Ja*, he had better admit that fact to himself, and be done.

Yet she stood motionless beside the hearth while he approached her and once more took her face between his hands.

"I think it does matter. How were you able to speak into my mind, Eadha?"

"I am what my folk call an empath. I feel other people's emotions whether I want to or no'. All but yours—I canna feel yours save when the madness is upon you. Then 'tis as if a door opens and I gain admittance to your mind."

Wonder flooded Tolljur. What a gift—and a curse almost as terrible as his own. And such a treasure to fall into his hands.

Very slowly he slid his hands from her face and threaded his fingers through her hair, just as he'd longed to do since he first saw her in Gunnar's hall. He waited for her to protest, but she made no sound. Instead she half closed her eyes and parted her lips.

An invitation? Surely not. Ties may well have formed between them, yet this woman—wed to another and longing for him—would scarcely welcome a berserker's attentions.

And he had promised not to force himself on her.

Yet this did not feel like forcing, especially when she raised both hands and placed the palms against his bare chest—not as if she sought to push him away but as if she might magically draw him in.

Breath held, he bent his head and gently brushed her lips with his, alive to her every reaction. Should she reject him even slightly, he vowed he would desist and not approach her again.

Liar. He would want this woman to his last breath.

Yet she did not pull away. Instead she tilted her chin and met his lips half way in a tender kiss, the merest brush of mouth to mouth that nevertheless felt like a flint striking against bedrock.

Need leaped up through Tolljur, almost as strong as the berserker rage—and every bit as unstoppable. He gasped as light exploded in his mind. She tasted of honey and fire and comfort so deep it terrified him. Somehow, though, he managed to hold himself.

Rarely did he hunger for a woman; such desire seldom escaped the iron control he kept so fiercely on his emotions. He stood ill prepared now for the ferocity of this hunger, provoked by her tender caress.

What to do with the emotion? Somehow he reined it in and gazed once more into Eadha's eyes. Wide with wonder and full of light, they suddenly filled his world.

"Eadha," he marveled, just as if he'd never before spoken her name.

"Tolljur," she returned and cast herself onto his chest.

The last threads of his control snapped with terrifying abruptness, even as need surged wildly and overtook his mind. He caught her tighter against him, clear off her feet, even as his mouth plundered hers, lips wooing and tongue searching. Searching for what? Her spirit? The other half of his own?

Her hands flew up from his chest and around his

neck, where they clasped tight. All sanity flown, his mouth fused to hers, he carried her to the bed.

He could see—feel—only one ending to this. Yet a woman such a she, he felt certain, must have the right to choose.

So when he laid her on his bed, he broke the kiss and asked raggedly, "Eadha, Eadha, will you accept me?"

Chapter Fourteen

Eadha, fast in the throes of emotions she barely recognized, struggled to get a grip on her desire. So this was that of which her friends back home had spoken when they longed for the marriage bed or, indeed, anticipated it. She had never expected such heat to beset her, but now…

Now she wanted this man, wounds, scars, madness, and all, as she had never imagined wanting anything, the desire wild and raw. She'd wanted him for days and—as she always got what she wanted—meant to have him now.

Yet such a joining would have ramifications. With the small measure of sense left to her, she sought desperately to identify them. The word *marriage* floated into her mind. Och, aye—he believed her married to another and would not expect her to be untried. She had to tell him. Now. Before.

Before her world shattered around her. For she sensed that if she lay with this man, nothing—nothing would ever be the same.

She unwound her arms from his warm neck and captured his face between her hands as he had hers only moments before. She had touched him while caring for him but never, never like this; his rough whiskers abraded her palms, and she could feel the deep seams of the scars on his cheeks.

A mere breath separated them when she said, "Wait."

Astonishingly, he did. She knew these men for plunderers—she had felt his companions' lust. By Lugh's heart, she wanted him to plunder her. She also wanted to give him the truth, so she gazed into his pale gray eyes and said, "I lied."

"Eh?" His grunt of surprise did not clear the haze of desire from his eyes. "What do you say?"

"I have no husband back home. I never had a husband. 'Twas a story I told to…to try and protect myself from Friti's lust. I am—untried."

"Ah, *ja*." Comprehension flooded through him visibly. By an effort so great it bunched his muscles, he eased away from her. "Then you will not want to finish what has started here."

Amazement filled her. Would he still withdraw and keep his promise? Had she found a man of honor in this place of demand?

Swiftly she told him, "I did not say that. Tolljur, I do want this. I want you."

Thoughts flickered in his eyes, like light and shadows on water. He froze in place, still leaning above her on the bed—his bed—deep with furs and redolent of his scent.

Och, and how could she hunger so for something she'd barely tasted? How long for something never had?

A terrible thought occurred to her. Perhaps he would spurn her because she had been untruthful—cast her off. Suddenly she could not breathe.

Speaking softly and steadily, he said, "Some men like to take what has not been gifted. Not me. I would be certain before I breach you, so that later you will not regret."

For most of Eadha's life she had longed to see the future, to divine it as had those druids and druidesses who'd come before her. She had begged Lugh for that gift and had found only the curse of empathy. Now she tried to gaze into her immediate future, to glimpse how giving herself to Tolljur Magnussen might change her life, and failed. She understood that pain would accompany the pleasure but did not know if disaster might also await.

As always when faced with such a decision, she followed her heart. "Take me, Tolljur. I will not regret."

Giving him no further chance to argue it, she reared up and fused her mouth to his. The taste of him flooded upon her, wild and so heady it immediately intoxicated her. Wanton with desire, she parted her lips and wooed his tongue into her mouth, wanting him more than breath.

She felt him succumb; his iron muscles eased, and he lowered his weight upon her, a delightful burden. The kiss, raw with need—both his and hers in equal measure—became all consuming.

Knowledge Eadha had never possessed sprang to her fingertips as she brushed his warm skin, as she explored both his and her own desire. His hands moved in response—everywhere at once—through her hair, down her neck and, with heart-stopping intensity, at her breast.

She broke the kiss then, even though it cost her in physical pain, and said, "Off."

"Eh?"

She felt his questioning and wondered when the

door had reopened in his mind—that which admitted her when he entered the throes of his madness. At some point during that mind-staggering kiss, she guessed.

"Nay, nay, nay," she admonished, marking each word with a little kiss to his mouth. "I am no' turning you from me. I want my clothing off."

Incredibly, he laughed. She had never before heard him do so. Now the sound traveled through her like the kiss of lightning and made her shiver. "Then we are of one mind."

"I want yours off as well."

"I am not wearing much."

"Even so."

He smiled at her as he heaved up, his gaze never releasing hers, and worked the ties on his leggings with one hand. The other, still at her breast, made short work of opening her bodice wide.

She half sat up and wiggled out of her other garments, devoid of shame or restraint. It seemed suddenly she had been waiting all her life for this—for him. Gladness enfolded her, mingling with the passion.

"Tolljur."

"Eadha."

Their names spoken and exchanged in claiming, heightened her emotions. She lay back on his bed in invitation. He feasted his gaze on her for a moment before he said, "I will do my best not to hurt you."

Eadha quivered from head to toe, like a chord struck on the harp in cadence with the music that filled her. Could she possibly be in love with this man?

Could she possibly not?

Holding his gaze, she returned, "I gift myself to you, Tolljur Magnussen. Do as you will."

"A priceless gift." Once more he cupped her breast with his hand, using his thumb to tease her nipple into a tight bud. "Know that me, I do not take it lightly."

He bent his head; his mouth found her breast, and she tumbled away into a maelstrom of passion.

His arms cradled her there, his body sheltered hers, and his spirit held and yet set hers free. She stretched wings never before unfolded, and flew.

His hands guided her, his lips coaxed fire from her veins. When she parted her legs for him, the desire became so fierce she barely noticed the fleeting sting of pain. The completeness, when they joined, chased everything else from her mind.

Did she breathe? Riding the last waves of riotous pleasure, she did not think so. She lay with arms and legs wrapped around him, staring at the rafters of the hut and wondering how she could ever again survive with him out of her sight.

For, strangely, coupling had ignited rather than satisfied her need. Och, aye, her body felt replete. Her spirit still wanted to hold him.

He had come to rest with his face in the crook of her neck. Now he stirred, and his hair trailed across her naked breasts, once more setting her alight.

He gazed into her eyes. "Did I hurt you?"

"Nay. Nay, you could never hurt me."

One corner of his mouth quirked up. She ached to kiss it. "I am berserker."

She repeated with emphasis, "You will never hurt me."

"How can you be so sure?"

How could she? Because she had been inside him even as he had been inside her. She had encountered and mingled with his spirit.

She raised a hand and caressed his cheek. He shivered in response, turned his head, and kissed her palm. She told him, "I am sure."

He reached again for her breast, fingers gentle and calloused palm abrading. He spoke a word in his tongue and repeated it in hers. "Beautiful. You have beautiful breasts."

Eadha, glad he thought so, nevertheless remained an honest woman. She had never been bonny and knew her body, slim and lithe, could not compete with the likes of Anaborg—lush and ripe with curves. Did that matter so long as he desired her?

She returned, "I also find you beautiful." She ached to reach for that tantalizing appendage between his legs, to wrap her fingers around its magical, silken strength, but did not quite dare.

He grimaced. "Me? Marked with old wounds. Scarred. Ugly." He indicated the still bandaged injury at his shoulder.

She told him with utter truthfulness, still gazing into his eyes, "You are magnificent."

He eased down beside her—satisfied?—his fingers still fondling her breast. Eadha's desire stirred more strongly and her emotions with it—that wantonness that surprisingly seemed to lurk just beneath the surface of her control. She felt content here with him, the intimacy reaching deep.

She wished this moment could last forever but knew it could not. And she still dared not contemplate what the future might bring.

Chapter Fifteen

Tolljur dreamed. In his dream he and Eadha stood together in Gunnar's great hall, in a patch of sunlight. Everyone he knew was there, witness to what took place between them. Eadha, dressed all in green with a golden necklace at her throat, wore her hair loose like a young maid, and she entrusted her fingers to his.

Tolljur remembered the necklace; his father had given it to his mother on the day they wed. His mother had long ago wrapped it up and given it to him, intending he should also present it to his bride on his wedding day.

Wed. In this dream, he and Eadha did wed.

Sure enough, he saw her lips move as she spoke the vows, echoing those he had already spoken. Then Kaddi, wearing his cloak of raven feathers, placed the cup of honey mead into his hands. He drank and passed it to Eadha, who also drank, but not before turning the cup so her lips touched the same place his had touched.

His mouth tingled in anticipation of kissing her, tasting her, claiming her once again. His bride.

He awoke to the silence of his hut, with his heart banging in his chest. Usually he dreamed of fire and pain, battle and the violence of the madness. He awoke sweating and filled with dread. Now he came to himself softly, the last strings of the bright scene stretching out from sleep to wakefulness like longing.

Warmth filled his arms. He became aware that he lay in his bed curled around Eadha, and she fast asleep. Her hand lay pressed against his chest and her breath came softly, fanning his skin like a caress.

Emotions he barely understood arose, rendering him at once humble and protective. Tenderly he drew her still closer and laid his lips to her temple.

She smiled but did not wake. He let the warmth and scent of her claim him once again and wondered what had happened to his life.

Much had happened, *much*. Control—ironically his one hope in the face of a madness that defied control—eluded him when he came to Eadha. With her, in coupling with her, he had shed restraint for the first time within easy memory and entered a place of profound intimacy. Passion, overcoming him, had found an answer in her passion.

He watched her sleep while doubt and certainty wracked him in turns. The dream, so different from those that usually beset him, had been a prophecy; he knew what he must do.

Yet how would she look at him when she awoke to the new day? It had not arrived yet—through the smoke hole above the cold hearth filtered only the misty light of the summer night. They need not face the future quite so soon. When morning came, when the enchantment between them broke apart, would she distrust him once again? He had taken from her the one thing he had promised not to take. But *nei*, she had freely given it.

He marveled over the woman he held in his arms: vulnerability and strength, magic and pragmatism, all in one form. And he wanted her again, as helpless against the desire as against the battle madness.

Yet he needed none of Kaddi's vile potions for this.

He kissed her softly, melding his lips to hers, still slightly swollen and tender. She sighed and stretched her legs apart in unconscious invitation.

"Eadha."

He whispered it, the merest suggestion of sound in the night. Somehow, she heard him and opened her eyes.

She smiled at him.

His heart convulsed in his chest, and his breath stuttered. Need beyond the physical seized him, that other want: to love and be loved.

Not for him, never for him. Yet he could almost believe what he saw in her eyes.

"Eadha," he repeated her name, "will you accept me again?"

She lay there gazing at him while she contemplated the question. He knew her now for an independent woman with a streak of self-worth that did not bow readily to slavery. And so, slave she would not be.

Except, perhaps—if she agreed to it—in his bed.

"Tolljur," she said and his name sang in his mind. "There is naught I will not give to you. Only ask."

Your hand, your heart—for eternity. But he did not say it. Instead he ran his fingers down her body, between her breasts and across her freckled belly and lower still, waiting for her to object. She did not, so he cupped the place, so damp and warm, that beckoned to him.

Her gaze never wavering from his, she opened her legs wider. He dipped one finger inside and then another, seeing the heat flare in her eyes. Desire began to hum through him like an echo of the music she played on her harp.

He said, admitting the desire, "I would taste you here—if you permit it."

Her eyes widened in surprise. Did she not imagine he wanted his mouth on her everywhere, in acts of barely expressible intimacy?

Slowly she said, "I gift my body to you, Tolljur Magnussen. Use it as you will."

And her heart? Did she gift that as well? But he did not ask, because she raised a hand and wrapped her fingers around his shaft, which stood for her, proud and strong.

The pleasure of her touch very nearly rendered him devoid of words. He stuttered, trying to remember her language. "*Nei*, but if you caress me so, I will have no time to taste you."

A wicked gleam invaded her eyes. Deliberately she ran her smooth palm up and down the length of him and asked, "Ah, then—would you have me stop?"

"*Nei*—for the love of Odin, *nei*."

"We ha' all night," she told him. "And tomorrow and the next day—" She broke off on a gasp as he bent his head and found her breast with his mouth. He lavished open-mouthed attentions there while he contemplated it. So her body was his to use, was it? A receptacle of his every desire? Let her only discover what that meant.

****

Suffused by emotions she did not understand, Eadha lay like a woman pinned to the bed while Tolljur worked his way down her body. She had never

118

imagined lying with a man could be like this. But coupling with him had been magical, an act involving both her body and her spirit. Offering herself again to him, like a sacrifice spread on stone, enflamed her.

Every part of her came alive to the hot ministrations of his mouth that moved ever downward, trailed by his hair that smelled of wood smoke and rampant male. He dampened her breasts, her belly and navel, and then the tender skin inside both thighs.

She felt his breath at that most intimate place where no man had been, save him.

His passion intensified, and her heart lifted. For aye, she had regained entry to his mind, to his spirit, when this madness—strangely similar to the other— overtook him.

He positioned himself and urged her legs farther apart; she could feel the callouses on his palms as they slipped beneath to cradle her buttocks. Utterly trusting, she lifted her hips in offering.

She felt the heat of his mouth make contact in the kind of kiss she had never imagined. Searing, demanding, consuming—he opened her and his tongue penetrated deep, invading her even as had that other magnificent part of him. Light exploded behind her eyes as she succumbed to the madness that overtook her in a strong wave.

Overtook them both.

She could not tell, after that, where his flesh began and hers ended, where his mind began, for she was with him there, experiencing both his pleasure and her own. When he moved back up her body and fused his mouth to hers, she tasted herself, a wild, heady flavor. When he plunged into her, she convulsed again.

He withdrew far too soon. She lay trembling beneath him, contemplating the way her life had shattered and come back together in a new form—one that required Tolljur Magnussen in it, the vital center of her existence.

They lay long while breaths and heartbeats calmed in unison. Outside, it began to rain, the faint shush of falling drops sounding distinctly in the stillness.

Tolljur stirred and drew Eadha more closely against his chest. Never had she felt so cherished.

She lifted fingers still sensitized and touched his face—explored the scars on both cheeks, traced the shape of his lips. Devotion filled her, strong and terrifying.

"Eadha." He spoke and his voice rumbled through her. "What was it Friti said to you before we left the bath house?"

Eadha struggled to identify Friti and recall any conversation. She belonged so completely to this man, all else flew from her. It took a moment before she admitted, "He said he would have me yet." She now understood just what that meant. The prospect of being taken by any other man made her shudder.

Tolljur, feeling her response, caressed her marked cheek with one calloused hand, and his lips brushed her forehead. "That is what I thought. You understand he wants to hurt me as much as he desires you."

She said with certainty, "'Tis he and not you who is the beast—bear shirt or no. What does he have against you?"

"There is a history between us. Old anger and jealousy."

"He envies you?"

"He envies my status, the honors in battle that sometimes place me before him." Tolljur laughed harshly. "He would not, if he understood the cost and what the trance takes when it comes. He wishes always to be first, Friti—in battle and with women."

"Well, he can never be first with me. You are first, for always."

He caught her hand and pressed his mouth to the palm, his only answer. Did he understand how she felt? How could he, since she barely understood?

Yet should he free her tomorrow, she did not know that she'd possess the strength to leave him.

Laura Strickland

Chapter Sixteen

"You look well." Kaddi gave Tolljur a discerning glance from his one remaining eye. "Better than you have in some time. What is it? Has the pain in your shoulder eased?"

"*Ja.*" Tolljur reflected upon it. The poison in his wound had abated—indeed, he had nearly forgotten the intensity of the ache. Eadha must have healed that last night, along with his spirit.

To be sure, she had magic of some kind—Gaelic or Norse, he cared not which.

It had come as a wrench to leave her behind and climb up the slope to Kaddi's hut. But he swore he could yet feel her with him.

To Kaddi he said, "I may need your help with something."

The old man straightened from the potion he had been busy stirring and gave Tolljur his undivided attention. "You know you have only to ask."

"I wish to make Eadha my bride."

"Eh?" Tolljur rarely saw Kaddi astounded, but he appeared so now. His brows flew up and his mouth dropped open. "Say that again."

"I wish to wed with her and so give her my protection."

Kaddi carefully set down the cup he held and swept Tolljur with another look, head to toe. "I suppose you

122

have taken her to your bed. That explains a lot. But wedding a slave—it is not done."

"It has been, in the past."

"Seldom enough."

"As I say, I wish to protect her. Making her my wife will do that."

"Ah, son, that is your cock talking. Where it has taken, it wishes to keep. But she is neither of your status nor your blood. You could demand far better."

Tolljur shifted his stance. "I do not want 'better.' Surely you have seen what she is. There is magic in her."

Kaddi raised his faded, blue eye to Tolljur's again. "There is, *ja*," he acknowledged. "In her own land I suspect she was a priestess—wife or daughter to a priest at very least."

"Not wife."

"So. It makes no difference. She follows not our gods and is not worthy of you."

"She can learn of our gods. Life is long. You could teach her."

Kaddi snorted. "The time remaining to me is not so long. What makes you think I would waste it on a southlander? Go home. Spend yourself on her, if that is what you need. Give her your seed—as to any bed slave—but *nei*, do not wed her."

"She needs the status of wife if she is to be shielded from Friti. As her husband, I will have legal recourse and a ready defense when I kill him, should he touch her."

Again Kaddi looked astonished. But he recovered and said, "You think so? Gunnar will never hear a blessed word against that son of his, whatever measures you take."

"Kaddi." Tolljur drew himself up. "I mean for her to be my bride. You can help me or hinder me, not both."

"Fool." Kaddi fisted his hands on his hips. "Of course you know I will help you. But it is no easy path you choose."

"I understand that."

"As for the woman herself—have you asked her? She just may possess spirit enough to refuse you."

"I know that also." Tolljur conceded it. "I shall need to persuade her, will I not?"

****

Tolljur, returning home, met with an incredible sight. The door of his hut had been pinned back, open to the softly falling rain, and dust flew out in billows. Eadha, it seemed, exerted herself on his behalf.

Upon that thought he caught a glimpse of the broom before she appeared, an intent expression on her face. Immediately the dull morning brightened.

She wore the new clothes Inger had provided for her, the gown a splash of dusty blue in the gloom, and had braided her shining brown hair neatly. With considerable concentration she chased the dust over the threshold before looking up and catching sight of him.

Her face lit and heat immediately filled her eyes. "Och, there you are—Master." A small, mischievous smile curled one corner of her mouth. "I wondered where you went."

"Off to see Kaddi." He indicated the pile of mingled dust and rushes. "What is all this?"

She shot him an innocent look. "I wish only to show how I mean to serve you…in any way I can." His

124

pulse leaped at the implications in her voice. "Only come inside and see. A fire burns in the hearth and your breakfast is ready."

"Is that all?" His arousal, immediate and intense, had him hard inside his leggings.

The heat in her eyes deepened. "Nay. Only come in and let me show you."

Like a man in a trance, he followed her in. She had not lied; a cheerful blaze brightened the hearth, and bread—only slightly burnt—stood on the stones.

Carefully, he tied the door shut and turned to find Eadha directly before him.

Gracefully, she sank to her knees. "Welcome home…Master."

By Odin's beard, how his blood leaped when she called him that name in that voice. Before he could draw breath to speak, she reached for the laces on his leggings. The smile tugged at her lips again.

"I thought I should give you a proper welcome."

Tolljur nearly convulsed as desire tore through him, straight from his groin outward. Did she know what she suggested? Apparently so, for she had freed him from his leggings and wrapped her fingers around him in an eager caress.

"Eadha—" he managed to croak.

"Would you rather have your breakfast first?" she asked, still with that mischievous innocence.

He growled, "I would rather have nothing else first. But—"

"I know fine how you pleasured me last night with your mouth and hoped I might return the favor. I ken what I want for my breakfast."

Wholly lost, Tolljur gave it to her.

****

"Eadha." Tolljur stirred sleepily on the rug beside the hearth and tried to remember something—anything—besides her name. She lay next to him, bare-breasted and with her hair loosened by his own hands. He had undone the braid after they moved across the hut to this nest, unable to take their mouths from one another. "That was a fine greeting."

"I only wish I could meet you so every time you come through that door."

"As do I." To his own surprise he laughed. "You would have me running errands a hundred times a day."

"And I always eager for you to come home." She stretched languidly, like a cat in the sun. "Who would have thought acting the part of a bed slave could be so pleasurable?"

"About that, Eadha, we must speak together."

Her eyes flew open. "You do not mean to cast me off, do you? Have I displeased you? Was I too bold?"

"You have displeased me in no way." He kissed her deeply, hoping to convey the feelings he could not otherwise express. "Though I want to keep you my slave no longer."

"Eh?" She stiffened.

Could it possibly mean something to her that she should remain with him? If so, by what miracle?

He ran his fingers through her hair and asked seriously, "It is not possible for me to cast you off, but if I did, would you not wish to return home?"

She went suddenly still. "I do not ken what remains there." She gazed into his eyes. "Do you remember that last battle, right before I was seized? Do you ken what became of my father—the chief? Friti faced him. But then I was dragged away and did not see..."

With real regret, he told her, "I very rarely recall aught that happens while I am in the grip of the madness. A flash here and there, a remembered image...that is all. I do not recall your father, and I do not know whether Friti slew him. I do know he has bragged much of his accomplishments on your shore and that few who face him live to tell the tale."

She squeezed her eyes shut, a woman in pain. "Ah, aye, I want to go home."

Tolljur's heart fell.

Swiftly she went on, "I do and yet do not wish to see how things stand there. I long to be with my family—those who remain. It feels like a betrayal, being here with you this way. Yet...a woman must survive."

"*Ja.*" Tolljur barely breathed the word. Was that all he meant to her? A means for survival? What more had he expected? He had no claim on her loyalty, nor her heart.

"You," she whispered, "are my enemy, are you not?" She opened her eyes and gazed directly into his. "Are you not?"

"I have no wish to be." He laid his palm against her cheek and went on softly, "Instead, I long to protect you. I find that is all I wish. Tell me again, and speak true: You are not wed in your land? No husband awaits you there? It was but a tale you told?"

"You must have felt the truth last night," she told him frankly. "I bled when you took me."

"*Ja.*" No other man had been before him. That did not mean she possessed a free heart. Did it matter? Women were forced all the time in many ways. Clearly he did not need to force her into his bed. Her morning greeting proved that.

He found, to his own surprise, he wanted both her body and her heart.

"Soon," he said, "Gunnar will once more send us off raiding. I will leave you then."

Her eyes darkened. With fear? Regret? Disquiet at what might happen if he and the other warriors returned to her land?

"Eadha, I would assure your safety from any who might think to use you in my absence."

"Friti," she said at once. "But surely if you go, he will go also."

"Maybe. Or in an effort to hurt me, to spite me, he may make some excuse to hold back from this voyage."

With the wryness so particular to her she said, "And miss all that bloodletting and carnage? Not he."

"Listen, this is a grave matter."

She touched his face in turn, a finger tracing one of the scars that marked his cheek. "Why does he hate you so? What trouble lies between you?"

Tolljur did not want to speak of Gyda. "It is an old quarrel based, as I say, in jealousy. It will come to a head one day—we must battle it out. I do not want it to be over you."

She trailed her finger down to his shoulder and lower still. "Why do we not flee together, then? You take me with you. We will find a new home in the world."

Ja, and just what did that mean? That she wished to spend the rest of her days with him? Surely not. Merely, she would trade even her body to him in exchange for freedom.

Well, he could offer her freedom of another sort.

Far more bluntly than he should, he blurted, "I wish for you to become my wife."

"Eh?" She drew back and stared, her hand dropping away from him.

Ah, and there he had his answer, he thought: she might indeed trade kisses—and more—for well-being, but it stopped short of linking herself to a scarred and blighted madman.

How could he have forgotten for even a moment? She had seen him in the throes of the madness.

He went on more carefully, "If we are joined—wed—before I go away, it will provide you the protection of my status and a measure of legal recourse should anyone threaten you. You will have rights not available to any slave."

"Och." It seemed all she could say for the moment. She lay there staring into the air—at nothing—her beautiful breasts rising and falling with her breaths.

"Have I the right to refuse?" she asked then.

Tolljur's heart sank still further, like a stone dropped into a bottomless pool. He struggled to master his disappointment.

"You have."

"But as a slave…"

"*My* slave. I give you that right."

She did look at him then. Her gaze searched and probed; he wondered what she saw. His desire for her to say "aye"? His longing, his need? When not in the madness, he had become adept at concealing his emotions behind this mask he wore. No reason to believe she could discern what lay beneath it.

Except for those wondrous moments when they

seemed to merge together and she climbed inside his mind, offering him strength, solace, understanding.

But now what did he see in her eyes, besides hesitance?

Abruptly she scrambled to her feet and turned away from him, catching up her dress, which she wrapped around her like a shawl. Tolljur, now feeling sick, rose also, shunning his own clothes, and stood watching her. Rarely had he felt so helpless.

"Eadha," he said hoarsely.

She turned and looked at him across the width of the hearth. Little tendrils of smoke rose up like wisps of magic, or spirit, making of her a mysterious vision.

"I ask this," he said, his voice still sounding rough, "only for your benefit—in an effort to shield you."

Her gaze moved slowly to inspect him once more, starting at his hair and moving downward as if she weighed her prospective bargain. Naked, he stood and hid nothing—scars, wounds or strengths—and held himself tight.

A small sound escaped her parted lips, softer than a sigh. "It seems so terrible final. I appreciate your trying to protect me, aye, but...if I accept you, 'tis like admitting I truly will never go home."

"If you refuse, I cannot promise to keep you from harm while I am away." In truth he could not promise it anyway. Nevertheless, if Friti ever moved against her, he, Tolljur, would have recourse to take the man apart with his hands as he so longed to do.

To his dismay, tears filled her eyes. *Ja*, he knew marriage for a bargain, often a matter as much of business as the heart. It did not require love.

Tolljur had never thought to propose it and now

that he had, he found he wanted far more than her agreement or even her loyalty. Yet when it came to this woman, he would take those if she would give no more.

He bade her, "Do not weep."

She palmed away her tears, mopping her eyes as inelegantly as a child. He waited for her to speak.

Please, Odin. Rarely did he pray, though he had as a boy: he had asked for strength and wisdom, for his father to come home safe. These days, he only uttered formula prayers before drinking one of Kaddi's potions and entering battle. Since Gyda's death, he had done no more.

Till now. He stood with his heart yearning, begging the great god for but one thing. The god answered through Eadha's lips. "Very well, Tolljur Magnussen. I will wed wi' you."

Chapter Seventeen

"Are you sure about this?" Catrin asked anxiously as she adjusted the folds of Eadha's fine gown. Catrin spoke in a tone too soft to reach the ears of Inger, who stood at the other side of the hut, arranging a ring of flowers meant for Eadha's hair. "'Tis not too late to back out."

Eadha looked into the face of her friend, which appeared pinched and slightly green. Morning sickness rode Catrin hard; the pregnancy with her master's child did not go easily.

Eadha said evenly, "I ha' no wish to back out."

She'd contemplated it for days, ever since giving Tolljur her assent. She'd examined the ins and outs of tying herself to this man—to this world—while she shook out his clothes, swept his hearth, and burned yet another batch of cakes. She had even crept outside once in the night while he slept, after they had loved each other with that intensity which seemed to overtake her so easily. She'd spoken then to Lugh and asked for wisdom.

Passion, as she well knew, had little to do with love. And swearing herself to Tolljur for the sake of mere passion—searing as it might be—would make her as mad as he became during a fit.

In truth, she did not understand what she felt for him. But she had only to touch him or look into his eyes in order to become swamped with emotion.

"I ken fine the marriage will be to your advantage," Catrin went on when Eadha did not elaborate. "But to him, of all men?"

Across the hut, Inger turned her head sharply. Did she hear after all?

Eadha, already taut with nerves, stiffened further. "Whisht! I remember fine how you warned me against him that first night when he claimed me, but, Catrin, he treats me well."

Right well, running his hot lips over her skin, enfolding her in his arms, and holding her so close against him that, at last, she felt safe.

"Aye, and you ever were heedless."

Eadha tossed her head. "'Tis not like home, is it? There I had a say in everything." Her da might have complained about what he termed her waywardness and her tendency to involve herself where she should not, yet he allowed her to speak always for what she believed.

Her heart twisted in her chest with the desire to see her home again, her da and mother. What would they say to this?

She argued against the homesickness. "Tolljur Magnussen offers me his protection this day."

Inger approached with the flowers in her hands. "What are you busy whispering about? Let me look at you," she added to Eadha. Inger wore an expression that signified dissatisfaction. Two wedding attendants, Eadha thought ruefully, and both disapprove of what I am about to do.

Inger's cool gaze swept Eadha before she said, "I hope you realize your good fortune, girl. You are not good enough for Tolljur Magnussen."

Eadha lifted her chin. Four days Inger had spent striving to talk Tolljur out of the union. Since it had all been spoken in Norse, Eadha had understood little; she did not have to. Inger's attitude said it all.

Inger had not been able to move Tolljur. Indeed, he had barely replied to her arguments. But when Inger at last departed, he took Eadha in his arms and chased away any doubt as to what he wanted.

She drew a deep breath, longing to see him now. Kaddi had taken him away, leaving her in the hands of these two.

She would not see him until they entered the chief's hall, where they would stand before the company and declare themselves husband and wife. They would also drink of the honey wine to seal the agreement. Both Tolljur and Kaddi had explained it to Eadha, but that did little to calm her nerves.

She did not like providing a spectacle for these folk, though she would if she must—if it meant Tolljur Magnussen would then be her husband.

She looked Inger in the eye. "You have made your opinion more than clear."

"I do not understand what sort of spell you have cast over him. Despite the madness he inherited, he is a practical man—levelheaded and not prone to doing such things as this." Inger huffed. "Take a slave for bride! I knew from the first there was something uncanny about you. You have bewitched him."

Catrin stirred uneasily, and Eadha willed her to remain silent. Catrin, like the other women captured from their isle, knew how hard Eadha had practiced at magic back home—the strength of her devotion to the holy path. This must seem as if Eadha now changed allegiance.

She did not; she had prayed to Lugh that she might forge a new way.

Gazing into Inger's face, she said, "I understand how much you care for him—like a son. And I promise I wish him no harm."

"No harm?" Inger seethed. "What sentiment is that for a wife toward her husband?"

"I also understand many—nay, most—of your unions are practical agreements and ha' little to do with love. Men—and sometimes women—take other partners on the side." Tolljur had explained that to her also, as he held her in his arms following lovemaking. Aye, well, even back home many a chief's daughter went into a loveless marriage to benefit her clan.

"But," she had told him there in the dark, "if ever you touch another woman—slave or otherwise—I shall take you to pieces with my bare hands. Even your bear shirt will no' protect you."

He had laughed, so rare an occurrence it moved her heart, and had held her tighter.

Longing to see him—painfully intense—accompanied the memory. To Inger she said, "Stop with your evil warnings and tell me how I look."

Inger's voice grew harder. "You are presentable. But your arrogance, my girl, will be your downfall. Just so you remember, you will *never* be good enough for him."

****

"You look uneasy," Kaddi murmured. "You are not going to tumble into a fit, are you? Perhaps you should drink this after all."

Tolljur spun to face the old man, and his fine cloak swirled around him. Not usually one to bother much with his appearance, he had nevertheless taken great pains this day, dressing in new leggings and a woven tunic with a golden amulet around his neck. He had parted his hair into a score of braids and Kaddi had fastened the sky-blue cloak with his own gnarled fingers.

"I will not tumble into a fit," he retorted, though he knew emotion, if extreme, could push him there. "And I want none of your potions this day." Kaddi had been pushing the goblet at him since he first arrived at the shaman's hut.

"*Ja*, you should. Just a mild mixture to calm you."

"I will go to my bride with a clear head." His bride. As always when he thought of Eadha, his heartbeat quickened. He had not seen her since dawn. And before that, when they lay together, he had asked her once more, "Eadha, are you certain?"

Ja and that had been Inger's fault, her days of warnings echoing in his ears. Gunnar had also taken him aside to ask, "Why would you wed your slave? You can have anything you want from her without taking that measure."

Their words started doubt in his mind where he had none on his own account—not that he did wrong in marrying Eadha but that she did wrong taking him for husband.

What woman wished to tie herself to a berserker—even in exchange for elevating her circumstances? For despite her assurances, despite her kisses, his heart still wondered if that made the true, the only reason she accepted him.

Of course, fool. What other reason could there be?

Kaddi grunted. "If you will not drink, we must go. You should be there awaiting your bride when she arrives."

"*Ja*. I look well enough?"

"Odin himself would be proud."

They walked down the slope together, the old man trailing Tolljur by a few steps. The day, soft with incoming clouds, threatened rain. A good omen that, Tolljur decided. The best unions were said to be blessed by rain.

It appeared the entire settlement had turned out for the joining. *Nei*—they would not wish to miss such a spectacle as the berserker taking his slave for bride. Unconsciously he drew himself up; he would present a composed front to all these onlookers, whatever might be going on in his head and heart, though he ached for a glimpse of Eadha.

If she did not come to him, his humiliation would be complete.

Gunnar stood already outside the door of the hall, with Friti beside him. The jarl looked solemn, Friti ready to start mischief if he could.

Gunnar stepped forward to greet Tolljur.

"Welcome, warrior, on this your bridal day. All honor to you in my hall." Gunnar's gaze probed him with what seemed like genuine concern. "Are you certain you would not rather postpone this until we return from our next venture? We leave in a mere seven-night—you will not have time for a full honeymoon."

"I would leave Eadha protected while I am away." Deliberately, Tolljur shifted his gaze to Friti.

Gunnar laid a heavy hand on Tolljur's shoulder. "Then I wish you the gods' blessings. Since you do not have your father present, would you like me to stand with you?"

"Thank you, but Kaddi will take that place."

"Then please to enter my hall."

Tolljur did; empty since everyone still congregated outside, it felt cool after the muggy air of the afternoon. His heart fell; *nei*, Eadha had not arrived before him. By Odin's eye—if she changed her mind, humiliation would be the least of his woes.

Someone had strung garlands of flowers above the place where they would stand. Kaddi, coming in behind him, shoved Tolljur beneath them.

"Go on," the old man grunted. "No time to falter now. And anyway, is this as frightening as entering battle?"

"*Nei*," Tolljur returned. It felt far more frightening.

Chapter Eighteen

"Courage," Eadha bade herself as she trod the narrow path afforded, between crowds of people, to the chief's hall. Somehow she had not expected so many onlookers, though she supposed she should have. As foremost among these warriors, Tolljur Magnussen made a figure of interest.

And on this day, he meant to wed a slave.

Eadha lifted her head still higher and reminded herself she was daughter to a chief, even if these folk knew it not. And she had never been lacking in self-worth. Still, she now trembled so hard she feared her knees might give way.

Catrin came behind her, silent. She reached out a hand when Eadha faltered upon seeing the doorway of the hall. The last time she'd been brought here, her life had altered drastically. It was, she knew, about to happen again.

The chief—jarl, so they called him—stood before the door with Friti at his side, both decked out in fine clothing and wearing silver amulets.

Please, Lugh, she prayed. With a nod for the chief and no further pause, she passed him and went in.

She'd intended never to set foot here again. Tolljur had not forced her to come with him on the occasions he feasted with the jarl. Other men, so she gathered, sometimes took their slaves with them as servers; in an effort to protect her, so she suspected, he had not.

She saw him waiting for her now across the hall, Kaddi at his side. Their eyes met and some of the tension drained from his body, allowing his shoulders to relax.

She had time for little more, for the crowd flooded in behind her, Gunnar and Friti first and the others behind.

Like a woman in a trance, Eadha paced across the floor to stand at Tolljur's side.

The hall had been fitted out as for some celebration—her wedding, she realized with shock. Tolljur had attempted last night to tell her what to expect, whispering in the dark. She had seen countless weddings back home but none in this savage place, and she would not be able to understand the words.

She wondered again what her father would say if he could see her now. Would he rage and protest? Would he forbid her taking an enemy—one of their fierce attackers—to husband? But her da did not know Tolljur Magnussen.

Upon the thought, she stole a look at him. And how well did she know him? Aye, she knew how it felt to lie with him—both thrilling and oddly safe—the flavor of him between her lips and the strength of his embrace. She knew too what befell him when the madness came upon him, for she had shared that. She had been inside him. But to swear away the rest of her life?

She swayed as her legs threatened to give way beneath her. Tolljur reached out and clasped her hand tight; at once she steadied. Her father might not approve; even if he still lived, he knew not what she faced here, and home lay at a great distance.

Gunnar began speaking then, and the crowd fell silent. Eadha could feel their eyes prodding and poking at her, merciless. She and Catrin were the only slaves present this day—a cruel irony that did not escape her.

Again she trembled, and Tolljur's thumb brushed the backs of her knuckles. In warning? In comfort?

No opportunity to decide. Gunnar stepped back, and Kaddi paced forward to take his place. The old man wore his cloak of raven's feathers this day and an amulet of gold with a large jewel that seemed to gather the light.

Eadha drew a breath; she recognized power when she saw it. For an instant, Kaddi's figure wavered before her eyes and she beheld Lugh's shining, silver form instead.

Power is power, Lugh whispered in her mind. *I am here.*

Kaddi looked up then and encountered her eyes. In her tongue he said, "That is why I shall repeat the instructions twice, out of courtesy to Tolljur Magnussen's bride.

"Tolljur Magnussen, do you freely and with a whole heart take this woman for your wife, solemnly and honorably in the presence of the All-Father?"

Tolljur's fingers seized on Eadha's. For an instant he gazed out at the crowd before hauling in his pale gaze and fastening it to her face. "*Ja,* with a whole heart."

Joy raced through Eadha, fierce and victorious. It made nothing of the watching strangers or the unknown future, or her own doubts. She watched an answering fierceness take hold in Tolljur's eyes.

Kaddi went on, repeating it in both tongues, "Do

you declare her your wife and you her husband?"

"I do so declare." Tolljur also repeated the vow in both tongues.

A ripple passed through the onlookers, but Kaddi did not pause. He turned to Eadha, his gaze kind, and spoke in Norse. He then asked her, "Eadha of the southlands, do you freely and with a whole heart take this man for your husband, solemnly and honorably in the presence of the All-Father?"

In the presence of Lugh, Eadha thought joyfully. She nodded and said, "Aye—with a whole heart."

"Do you declare him your husband and you his wife?"

"I do so declare."

Kaddi also nodded. When Eadha once more looked at Tolljur, he held a gold necklet. Very carefully, he placed it over her head, the scarred backs of his hands brushing her hair. It lay upon her breast, glowing softly with amber.

Kaddi turned to those gathered and spoke at some length. Catrin, a carved goblet in her hands, stepped forward from Eadha's side and offered the cup first to Tolljur.

Kaddi spoke in Eadha's tongue, "Drink you together and share this mead as you will henceforth share all of life—drink, bread, joy, and sorrow. Let it seal your union."

Tolljur, his gaze fixed on Eadha's face, raised the goblet and drank. For an instant Eadha fancied she tasted the honeyed drink with him, as if his strong emotions once more drew her inside him.

He had explained this part also—and the significance of drinking the honey wine together.

Couples repeated this part of the ritual for a full month during their honeymoons.

Tolljur placed the cup in Eadha's hands. He had instructed her to turn the goblet so her lips found the place his had rested. She would have wanted to do that anyway, eager for even the echo of his caress.

She drank, the sweetness flooding upon her, and Kaddi held up his hands. He spoke in Norse now, the words celebratory. But no one cheered; instead, weighty silence met whatever pronouncement Kaddi had made.

Catrin relieved Eadha of the goblet, and Kaddi turned to Tolljur and clasped his arm. He then smiled into Eadha's eyes. "Be good to him, child, and he will be good to you."

"Aye. Thank you."

And so—as simply as that—was she bride to Tolljur Magnussen? Yet not so simple. There was supposed to be a feast of celebration following this; indeed, the tables had been moved into place and even now stood ready. But no one there appeared joyful.

Even the light faded rapidly as the clouds outside thickened. Distant thunder rumbled, and Tolljur once more claimed Eadha's hand.

He said something in Norse to the company, then added for Eadha's benefit, holding her hand high, "Thor himself is present and roars his approval of this joining!"

Those in the hall exchanged glances; a few heads bowed and still fewer fists raised. Eadha heard the name of the god—Thor—repeated before the storm came upon them in earnest, rain crashing and thunder beating the roof of the hall like a skin drum.

At that moment Tolljur turned to Eadha. His pale gaze engaged hers before he bent his head and claimed her lips in a kiss so deliberate it became a declaration. The taste of him invaded her, mingled with the sweetness of the honey wine, and for an instant her heart stilled.

How could she hope ever again to live without this man?

****

The storm faded to a steady rain, the feasting ended, and the celebration—such as it was—waned. Tolljur had warned Eadha what might come at the end of it: once the ale and mead had flowed sufficiently, the wedding guests sometimes took matters into their own hands and bedded the bride—took her to her husband's hut, stripped her of her finery, and placed her between the sheets. The groom would be ushered in, likewise stripped, and showed to her.

Sometimes the guests even stayed to observe a successful mating.

No great matter, she tried to tell herself, in a community that took such mating as a matter of course. Had not Catrin told her those who lived in common halls copulated within each other's hearing and sight? And had Catrin not been deflowered so by her new master, within the hearing of others?

Yet it seemed no one among this company had the heart for such jibes tonight. Inger, like so many others, had spent the evening glaring at Eadha in disapproval. Anaborg, a tight, sour look on her face, had left, as had Friti sometime later, and though Gunnar remained, he looked restless.

At last Tolljur arose from the head table and gave

144

Eadha his hand. "Come, wife."

She rose. The strong drink had gone to her head, and her husband's face wavered before her eyes.

He seemed to consider her state, gave a rare smile, and swung her off her feet, up into his arms.

A few cheers greeted the spectacle of him bearing her from the hall. He carried her out into the rain, which still pounded down with a force like plunging knives.

Tolljur lifted her higher and sprinted. She wound her arms around his neck and tucked her face beneath his chin.

Someone—Inger?—had lit the fire in their hut, and the warmth felt welcome. The hut, quiet and sheltered after the noise of the hall, beckoned them in with shadowy arms.

Without pausing, Tolljur carried her to his bed.

Chapter Nineteen

Tolljur peered into the face of his new wife, barely visible in the shadowed hut. Despite his care and hurry, rain had soaked her hair and fine green gown, and now glittered on her face. He felt wet to the bone and could still hear the rain crashing down on the ground outside.

He needed to strip off his wet clothes—and hers. Tipsy as she was, he should tuck her into the furs and let her sleep. Yet he'd ached to take her from the moment she had entered Gunnar's hall, and this was his wedding night.

Ja, he thought ruefully, and was he a rutting beast who could not control such urges?

He stepped away from the bed, and Eadha reached out and snagged his hand. Her fingers felt wet and chilly, her grip tenacious.

"Where do you think you are going—husband?" She breathed the last word in a manner that had the blood rushing through him and his heart beating wildly.

"To secure the door. We want no visitors set on playing pranks this night."

She sat up as he moved off, her gaze fastened to him. "We do not."

When he returned, she arose, still swaying slightly, and moved into his arms. "I would have nothing disturb us this night."

Heat suffused him at the feel of her so close against

him. She lifted her mouth to his, and he took it ravenously, the way a drowning man takes air. She tasted of the rain, the mead that had accompanied their feast, and the wild, womanly flavor that was hers alone.

She broke the kiss and drew away far too soon. They gazed into one another's eyes.

She seemed to search him for something; he felt her awareness probe his heart and mind. What would she ask from him this night? He wondered suddenly. More than he was prepared to give?

But she said only, "You looked so handsome when I entered the hall earlier."

Surprise shot through him. He had been called many things—never handsome. Yet he sensed no lies in her.

"And you," he returned. "So lovely." The words seemed terribly inadequate. Eadha's singular appearance had no equal among other women. With her freckles and stark bone structure, he had first supposed her plain. Now he knew her beauty extended far beyond what he could see, to what he could *feel*.

Solemnly he said, "I hope you are not disappointed in your groom."

"Disappointed? Tolljur Magnussen, I have traded my future to you along with any hope I had of returning home. I am willing to spend my life here among strangers for your sake. Does that sound like disappointment?"

Struck humble, he did not know how to reply. Used to being at once the best and worst of men, he'd never expected to command any woman's heart.

"You do not believe me," she observed, still gazing into his eyes. "Let me show you."

Her hands moved to untie the front of his tunic. Just like that he arose for her, high and hard. The gods—bless them—had sent him this gift. Should he ask why?

She said, gently chiding, "You are supposed to undress me as well."

He reached immediately for her hair and hesitated. "How does this come undone?"

She laughed softly and heat rushed through him in a blaze of fire. "You think first of my hair?"

"I love your hair."

Her hands, now inside his tunic and damp against warm skin, froze. Her eyes questioned him. She had not expected to hear that word this night; he had never intended to speak it, yet here it came already, issuing from his lips.

Did he love his new wife? More than her lovely, shining hair, more than those breasts that seemed made to fit in his hands, the long legs and the well of heat between them?

Could he fail to love her? Oh—Odin save him!

"First you," she whispered. "Then me."

"Eh?"

Without further words, she drew the loosened tunic over his head. She used her mouth to gather the moisture from his chest and worked her way southward through the hair that trailed down his belly, where she paused to untangle the ties on his leggings. She stripped him slowly and deliberately, her mouth following her hands everywhere, denuding him of everything but his golden amulet. When he stood in only that, she pushed him backward onto the bed.

Without pause, she then began removing her own

clothing, allowing the damp garments to fall at her feet. Tolljur, beyond aroused, watched through hazy eyes, and when she stood naked to his gaze, but for the necklet his father had given his mother on their wedding day, he growled and reached for her.

"Uh-uh!" She danced back a step, her fingers reaching to unfasten her hair. "I would have everything just the way you want it this night…husband."

He reminded himself of all the drink she had taken, and assured himself that even though he might indeed love this woman he had no cause to believe she loved him in turn. She had merely struck an advantageous bargain today, the only one available to her.

But when she at last joined him in the bed, when her damp hair swept across his skin and her body met his, he did not care.

Kisses, firelight, heat, and his new wife's mouth all over him—those eclipsed all else. There seemed to be no act she would not perform this night, and eagerly. She anticipated Tolljur's desires, moved to satisfy them almost before they formed in his mind, and the need in his flesh turned to something far deeper.

It frightened him there in the dark, how his emotions—always held so tight—opened and let her in. It terrified him, trying to imagine ever again living without this woman because life, as he knew it, was all about loss. Days might be had, and nights in her company—not eternity.

Long after the fire in the hearth died—the one inside him lasted far longer—and the rain softened outside, she stirred and crawled up his body to his lips. She kissed him long and languorously, and he tasted himself in her mouth, fierce and strong.

"Well, husband," she whispered, "and are you satisfied?"

Was he? By Odin's eye, he should be. Even at the prodding of his desire—which seemed astonishingly imaginative—he could not think of another way to take her. And she so willing. More than willing. In fact, had she not contributed a few ideas?

She laughed, and her fingers, bold with the intimacy of possession, moved down his body and closed about his member. "I see you still have strength to stand."

"Only near you," he murmured. "In battle I would be weak as a kitten."

"Ah, but this is no' battle."

"What is it, then?"

She seemed to contemplate the question even as her fingers caressed him gently, coaxing an effortless response. She leaned closer and whispered into his ear, "It is magic."

"Must be. You have drained me dry."

"And will again. Your flesh is mine, and my flesh is now yours—'tis the way of things between man and wife."

"Is it?"

"For me, aye. I know nothing about other folk's ways."

She pressed her body against him, and he gathered her in, snagged one of the covers—the only one he could still reach—and swaddled them both. For the first time in memory, he felt at peace.

Only let me die so, he prayed to his gods, here with her, not out on some cold shore. But he was berserker, meant to die in battle the way the wind dies in storm.

And he'd been taught no glory lay in a man dying in his own bed. Ach, but who cared for glory?

"I wish," she went on softly, "we need never emerge from this place."

"And I."

"Truly?" She wiggled about until she could gaze into his eyes. "Would you be content with just me?"

"'Just' you?" he repeated and ran his fingers through her hair for the sheer pleasure of it. He knew her now; she was full of life, winsome and intelligent, with a deep spirit and a mind full of twists and turns, all of which he might never discover. He knew at that moment he would live forever in her, if he could.

Yet he possessed little skill with words and less with her language. He said only, "Truly."

"You would not grow bored, with only me?"

"Bored?" To his own surprise he began to laugh, helpless with it. "Bored does not come close to mind when I think of you, Eadha Magnussen."

Wickedly she demanded, "What does come to mind?"

"I have already shown you."

"Well, show me again."

"How?"

"Any way you like, though I do have a powerful craving for the taste of you in my mouth."

Did she? And the mead long worn off. His lips curled. "I would hate to disappoint my new bride."

She began moving down his body, trailing her hair as she went, until she positioned herself between his legs, spreading them slightly. "Somehow, husband, I do not think you will."

****

Eadha awoke with but one thought in her mind.

Tolljur.

Even before she opened her eyes, she reached for him. Her mind stirred, then her fingers, and then her desire.

How could she possibly want him still? She recalled—quite vividly—all that had occurred during the night. The ways she had enjoyed him, and he her. The number of times. It must have been a mad dream, because she, Eadha MacEwan, could not possibly have acted with such abandon.

Eadha Magnussen now, she reminded herself. She had done the unthinkable—amid all the other unthinkable acts—and married the berserker, enemy of her people, monster, madman...

And where was he, this husband of hers? For her searching fingers met only empty bed. Warm, but still...

Her eyes flew open on a surge of panic. She could not go on breathing if she did not find him.

Her frantic gaze located him not far away, hunkered down and trying to coax a fire in the cold hearth—naked, and utterly perfect to her eyes.

Ah but could he be considered perfect? She narrowed her gaze. Scarred, aye—and still bearing that last batch of wounds. She watched the way the plaits he'd made in his light brown hair fanned across his back when he moved and the play of muscles in taut buttocks. Perfect for her.

"Where is my honey wine?"

He straightened and spun, startled at the sound of her voice. She let her gaze caress the front of him with lazy pleasure.

Hers.

A smile came to his face, effectively distracting her from other delights. Tolljur Magnussen smiled so seldom. Perhaps she should make it her life's work to persuade more such from him.

"Honey wine for breakfast?" he questioned.

Och, and the sound of that voice. It trembled through her the way a harp string trembled through a song, starting a beautiful response. She recalled the sound of it murmuring all last night while she gave and gave, without restraint.

She propped herself up on her elbows, breasts bare, swollen and tender amid a tangle of her own hair. "'Twas my understanding we are to drink of it together every day for a month."

His smile dimmed slightly, and stark gravity descended on him. Nay, she thought. Let him not change.

But he returned lightly, "First thing in the morning?"

"Aye. And then I get to have my way with you."

The smile returned with a flash. "Your way? That might well kill me."

"I do no' think so. Husband, are you no' meant to answer my needs? I am lonely here, and cold."

"So, do I not strive to awaken the fire?" He gestured to the hearth.

"My fire is quite awakened, I assure you."

He abandoned his task and approached the bed.

"Do no' forget the mead," she reminded. "I believe I would like my portion poured over your body. I will lick it off."

He froze, then snagged the jug of honey wine

153

before continuing to the bed with new determination.

"That sounds interesting."

She allowed her gaze to fondle him once more. "I can see your interest. You drink first."

He carefully unstopped the vessel and took a drink. Eadha, accepting the jug from him, placed her lips where his had been.

"Ah—the day begins. And I ken fine, husband, how we will pass it."

"Eadha," he told her gently and with some regret, "there is a world beyond this hut."

"Aye, but it is out there and we are still in here. Let us make this time last as long as we can."

Chapter Twenty

Tolljur could no longer remember how many days he and his new wife had been together in his dwelling, nor guess how soon he was meant to leave for raiding. The time, a jumble of light and darkness, honey wine and pleasure sharp as pain, had merely slipped by with no relation to reality. He now believed completely in magic—the sort woven by his wife. He no longer knew where her desire ended and his began. He belonged to her as he had never imagined belonging to anyone.

And he swore he could feel the thoughts in her mind, knew what she wanted and how. The newly developed ability seemed reciprocal. No more did he think of feeling her mouth on him in a certain place than she applied it there.

Now he awoke from a deathlike sleep, full of fathomless peace, because she stirred and applied those lips to his ear.

"Husband."

Lust—pure and powerful—thrilled through him. She had only to speak that word.

Yet bright sunlight poured through the roof vent—how many days since they had kindled a fire?—and with it some sense.

Had they eaten? Food, that was. How long could they exist off one another?

Ja, well, there was the honey wine. And he

remembered her dropping some sort of cake into his mouth at one point. A new emotion passed through him. He suspected they had emptied the last jug of mead.

"I ha' a question."

Of course she did. The woman's mind never stopped moving, her curiosity and intelligence both far-reaching.

Thank you, Odin, he thought and not for the first time.

He smiled and turned his head to find her lips within reach of his. Time suspended as so often when he kissed her.

He decided he would have her breasts for breakfast followed by…

But she broke the kiss. "Question."

"Speak it."

She ran her fingers through his hair, which she'd unbraided at some point, as if she owned it—which she did—and gazed into his eyes. "Why do you so seldom leave your seed inside me?"

"What are you talking about? I do." He could taste himself now within her mouth. But he knew what she meant, and his heart thudded.

Her gaze—hazel flecked with gold and green— held his, inescapable. "Sometimes, aye, but not there inside my womb where I want you."

"You want me everywhere."

"True." She dismissed that, though. "But you usually withdraw from there at the last, before your seed comes. Why?"

Could he lie to her? Ever? No.

"I do not wish to leave you a child."

Her gaze cooled, and he felt her withdraw. "Why? I can think of little better than bearing your bairn."

He returned softly, "I can think of little worse than giving you one. Especially a son." He sought to explain. "I am berserker. Do you forget?"

"I do not forget."

"And my father was berserker before me. Chances are good my son would be berserker."

"It is an inherited gift?"

"Curse."

"I see." Clearly she did. Doubt and dismay warred in her eyes. "You mean never to give me a child?"

"We should have spoken of this before we wed. A woman has a right to *kinder*. You would not have accepted me had I told you."

"Tolljur Magnussen, I would ha' accepted you even had the result left me blind. Can you not tell that by now?"

He had hoped. But he feared a woman's mind could not be measured by passion—even such a passion as hers.

"I supposed I left you satisfied without my seed," he offered.

"You do leave me satisfied." She kissed him fiercely. "And vastly unsatisfied, it seems. One of life's great mysteries. I simply canna get enough of you." She hesitated. "Are you certain your child would inherit the madness?"

"*Nei*. But I will not take the chance."

"Yet I would like a part of you to carry inside me."

His heart nearly spasmed in his chest. "Would you?"

"Aye. Catrin—you know she is to bear her

master's bairn?"

He shook his head.

"She says the longing for home becomes more bearable once one has a child."

He caressed her hair. "You long for home still?"

"Sometimes I am sick with longing. Alba is in my blood and bone."

"I cannot send you home." He would gladly do almost anything else for her—save give her a child. But he could not live without her. The very thought stole his breath.

"I know."

"It is not done. And anyway…" Tell her, his mind urged. Give her something in place of the child she will never hold.

Yet could his paltry heart—that of a berserker—make up for empty arms?

She tipped her head. "Anyway?"

"I leave. Soon." It must be soon. He could scarcely believe no one had yet come calling at his door, least of all Inger.

"Leave?" she repeated stupidly.

"Go back to sea. Raiding."

She said nothing, but suddenly a stranger looked at him from her eyes.

Protesting the change in her, he said, "You knew this would come when you took me to husband."

"I knew, aye. But perhaps I hoped I might change your heart."

His heart, as he was well aware, lay squarely in her possession.

She rushed on in that way she had. "Can I not persuade you from continuing to kill my people?"

Was that what all this had been about? All the kisses, the warmth, the welcoming—mere attempts at persuasion?

He sat up in the bed, bringing her with him. "This thing I cannot change."

"Are you certain?"

"*Ja*, I am certain."

"There is nothing I can do…?"

He caught her between his hands. "*Nei*, wife. Nothing."

And what did he see flood her eyes? Consternation? Regret?

He shook himself slightly, like a man surfacing from deep water. "I must go forth, discover when we are meant to depart. And prepare my weapons. I cannot believe even Kaddi has not been to the door."

"Are folk here in the habit of interrupting a honeymoon?"

"*Nei*. But he usually begins giving me the potions days ahead of time."

"These potions—what effect do they have on you?"

"Different effects." He crawled out of the bed and began to search for his clothing. "Some lend me strength. Some make the madness come more readily."

"Why would you want that?"

He paused and gazed at her. "Because in battle I may be taken by the fit many times in succession. If I fight against it, there is a cost to be paid, after."

He turned back, found his tunic—the one he had worn to his wedding—and a single boot.

"I do not like you being under the influence of such potions. I say you should stop."

"Eh?" He paused again and stared at her. "Stop?"

"Being a berserker." She waved a hand regally. "Leave it alone. Do something else."

"Something else?" He did not know when he had been so surprised. "It is not something I *do*. It is what I *am*."

"I do not think so." She shook her head, the chestnut hair flaring around her. "I have felt what you are, tasted it—learned it. 'Tis no' a berserker."

The boot fell from his suddenly nerveless fingers. "You know not of what you speak."

"I say again—I know you, Tolljur Magnussen."

She too climbed from the bed and walked toward him without regard for her nakedness. When she reached him, she twined her arms around his neck before pulling herself up to curl her legs about his hips.

"Kiss me. And tell me you will go to fight no more."

So that *was* what she wanted. Consternation flooded him in turn. She had spent all these days seducing him only to steal his sting. His purpose.

He shook his head, even as his hands shifted instinctively to support her bottom. "I cannot."

"Kiss me." Not waiting for it, she nipped one corner of his mouth and licked his lips, seeking admittance.

Somehow he managed to resist and stared her in the eyes. "*Nei*. You do not understand."

Very carefully he set her down and pushed her a step or two back.

"So." She tossed her head. "You will go back to that old man—he with the raven cloak—and drink his poison? Have you ever asked yourself how much of your madness is prompted by his potions and not what is inside you?"

"*Ja.*" He had considered it. "But Kaddi is a good man with my best interests at heart."

"You believe that?"

"I do."

She asked with a hint of challenge, "You say he serves Odin—that is the god you also follow, is it not?"

"Odin is foremost among them. And *ja*—Kaddi follows him in his search for purity and wisdom." He tugged the tunic over his head and added, "Did he not put out his own eye in an effort to emulate the All-Father?"

"What?" She stared. "And these folk call *you* mad? How did he do it?"

"I do not know. He went away on a pilgrimage and came back like that. This happened when I was but a child."

"You never asked him how a man does such a thing to himself?"

"One does not intrude between a man and his gods. Or do you not give credence to such?"

She went very still. "I give it credence."

"I must go." He climbed into his leggings, wondering if he could truly force himself back out into the world, if things would be the same when he returned later. Would she welcome him back again? Would the magic woven between them hold?

Regret and doubt in equal measures squeezed his heart. And for the first time in days he turned away from her and opened his door.

Chapter Twenty-One

"Everyone is talking about you. How you have married the berserker and been shut away with him for days." Catrin flicked Eadha with a concerned look. "Are you all right?"

Eadha drew a breath and narrowed her eyes against the bright day. It felt as if she had just returned to life after a long, enchanted sleep. The world seemed too loud, too glaring—not quite real. What mattered lay in the dim air of the hut, that which had passed between her and her new husband.

"He did not hurt you?" Catrin pressed. "When no one saw either of you for so long, it was whispered he had killed you in a fit and would not come forth."

Eadha focused on her friend's face. "What nonsense."

Catrin shrugged. "'Tis what we feared and the reason why female slaves would rather go to the common men than fall into his hands. I did warn you."

When Eadha said nothing, Catrin leaned closer and asked, "What were you doing in there so long?"

"What do you suppose?"

Catrin withdrew slightly. "He forced you?"

"Nay. He is my husband."

"Not by your choice, surely. He is berserker—a madman."

Eadha had no chance to reply; Inger came storming

up the hill, kerchief on her head and arms akimbo.

"At last you see fit to emerge!" she greeted Eadha. "Where is your husband?"

Catrin moved off quickly, head down. Eadha turned to meet Inger's glare.

"Tolljur has gone to speak with the jarl and see when he must depart on the longship."

"And you stand here idle, not even a broom in your hands. I suppose that house is a midden inside. Why are you not busy cleaning?"

Eadha ignored the criticism. "Do you know when the longships will depart?"

"Two days. You spent nearly seven pent up in there together."

Two days. Eadha's heart sank like a stone. She tried to untangle the emotions that swamped her, and failed.

Inger glared harder. "What kind of wife will you make for Tolljur? No smoke has come from this hut in days. Have you shaken out the bedding? Emptied the piss pot? Prepared his bread?"

"Nay, nay, and nay."

"I ask again what sort of wife—"

"The one he chose. The one he wants."

Inger's gaze scalded Eadha's face. "Arrogant, you are. That arrogance will be your downfall."

"How many women sweep their hearths during their honeymoon?"

"Those worth their salt. Anyway, you are different—you are wife *and* slave. Have you forgotten all I tried to teach you?"

"Nay, but you were no' so unkind then."

"I did not expect you to usurp the place of your

betters. A bed slave is one thing—wife another."

"I care little for what you think," Eadha retorted, perhaps unwisely.

"You should care. Your friends are few enough— your enemies numerous. They will make mischief for you if they can."

"What enemies?"

"Anaborg Helmsdottir, for one. She is going about saying she should have been Tolljur's wife, that you must have cast some enchantment on him to make him take you—and to keep him here with you so many days."

"She is naught but a shrew."

"*Ja,* but she has powerful connections. It is rumored she spent the night before last in Jarl Gunnar's bed."

"In whose bed has she not been?"

"I will not argue that question with you. Come, let us see the disaster within, and I will help you clean before Tolljur returns."

"Nay—I have no time." Eadha's eye had caught a flash of black, the old man moving about higher on the hill. "I must go speak with Kaddi."

"You come back here," Inger called, even as Eadha lifted her skirt and began to climb.

Inger's voice died away behind, sounding like the screech of the seabirds from the shore. Eadha followed the path through the green turf, aware that those she passed stared, and she called to Kaddi when she neared.

The old man paused and looked at her. Slightly breathless, she reached him and said, "Have you a moment? We need to speak together."

"*Ja.* Come in."

The interior of the old man's hut smelled pungent and clean. Not for the first time Eadha wondered what he put in the potions he brewed both for Tolljur and others. She sensed the vestiges of magic here as well, and power.

The same sort of power she herself had sued, back home.

She could not let that sway her now. She lifted her chin, looked Kaddi in the eye, and said, "I ha' come about Tolljur."

"*Ja*, so?" Kaddi set down the bucket he carried and faced her. "Say what you will."

"I want you to stop dosing him."

Kaddi laughed. "Repeat that, girl. I must have heard you wrong."

"I want—"

Swiftly he interrupted. "What do you know of it? Think you own him, do you, after spending a few days in his arms?"

Eadha sought to grapple with her reaction. Anger would get her nowhere. "I have no quarrel with you, Master Kaddi. I hope we both want the same thing: what is best for Tolljur."

Kaddi laughed again, a rough chuckle this time. "Am I to put faith in your concern? You come here a slave and within the course of a single moon you are supposed to have granted your allegiance to your master?"

"Not master. Husband."

Kaddi's eyebrows flew up. "Am I to suppose your heart is involved?"

Eadha took a hard look at it and, with difficulty, admitted, "It is."

"So—you think you love him?"

"I did not say that." Eadha doubted she understood love; she had never expected to experience it beyond the devotion she felt for Lugh.

"Then what *do* you say?" Kaddi challenged.

She shook her head. "My feelings are so stirred, I barely recognize them. But you can believe that I act out of genuine concern for him."

"As do I—and have since he was a boy. I served his father before him, until his death."

"These potions you mix—what is in them, and what is their purpose?" She had asked Tolljur but wanted it from the old man's lips.

"Are you an herbalist, girl?"

"Nay."

"Then I can tell you, but you will not understand."

"Neither am I a fool. He says…" She paused weightily. "You begin preparing him with draughts well before the company leaves to go raiding."

"*Ja.*"

"Why?"

Kaddi sighed. "His body is not like those of other men." His single eye flashed. "And I do not doubt you have depleted him with your recent excesses. When in a berserker fit, great strain is placed upon his heart, his muscles, his mind. It is how his father died."

"I thought he was clubbed in battle."

"So he was—struck down in the middle of a fit. But being struck did not kill him. He lasted days after they brought him home. I examined him then and know the truth: his heart exploded."

"What?" Eadha backed off a step, and dread washed over her such as she'd never known, even when faced with capture.

She could not bear to lose Tolljur that way, or *any* way. She simply could not.

"But…but his father was an older man—that will not happen to Tolljur."

Kaddi shrugged. "Who knows? The madness, as I say, exacts a high price. And he will do no better for missing the fortifying drinks he should already have taken." Kaddi paused and seemed to consider Eadha before he went on. "His father had been away raiding many days, and he sometimes forgot to drink his potions. He had only thirty-six winters when he fell. Tolljur has nearly thirty now."

Tolljur, flesh of her flesh, bone of her bone. Eadha took a deep breath. "Tell me how I can keep him from going away to fight."

Kaddi laughed once more. "You cannot."

"Then tell me of these various drinks you brew for him. I would still know what is in them."

Again the old man seemed to consider it. He nodded. "There are three he takes. The first, as I say, prepares him in body and mind, and gives him strength."

"Body and mind? It affects his mind?"

"Perhaps I should say 'spirit.' Your tongue trips me, girl."

"The second?"

"To be taken on the day of battle, as close as possible. It lowers the barriers."

"He said something about making the fits come easier, but I do no' understand."

Kaddi gave her a hard look from his single, faded eye. "I agree; you do not. That is why—"

Rudely Eadha interrupted, "And the third?"

"A restorative. Human flesh, bone, and sinew can endure only so much."

Spurred by those feelings she barely comprehended, Eadha began to pace. "Are you certain, Master Kaddi, this second potion of yours does no' cause the fits rather than ease them upon him? I think perhaps you seek to control Tolljur, perhaps to win favor with your chief."

Kaddi gave a bark of laughter. "I curry no favor with him."

"With your gods, then." She whirled to face him. "I ha' known men like you before—so much focused beyond this world they would trade away all in it. But Tolljur Magnussen is no longer yours to trade. He is mine."

And what prompted her to make that declaration?

"Sit down," Kaddi told her sternly.

"But—"

"Sit."

To Eadha's own surprise, she did. Kaddi came and perched opposite her, his expression kind.

"List to me, girl. You may be flush with the heat of honey wine and the things you two have been doing together, but he is not yours. Nor mine. He belongs, as ever, to the gods. I do nothing to harm him. Do I not love the boy as if he were my own?"

Eadha's heart fluttered with panic. "But this second potion of which you speak, that 'lowers the barriers'— why? Is it not terrible enough that the madness must come upon him and steal his will? And him powerless against it—why would you encourage that?"

"You have just said: he is powerless against it. I

was friend to his father, Magnus. From boyhood I watched him struggle with the fits, seek to cope with them, live through them. I spoke to Odin. I sought wisdom." He gestured to his face. "I sacrificed much and was given the means to help my friend. And his son after him. Would you truly doubt me?"

Taken aback, Eadha eased up on her aggression. "Forgive me, Master Kaddi. I do not mean to. It is but that I now have a need inside me. To protect him."

"Good." Kaddi spoke the word gruffly. "He needs that. But be aware your heart cannot alter what he is—berserker first, all else including husband to you second."

"Explain to me, please. He inherited this curse from his father?"

"*Ja*, and this you must understand: it will come upon him whether he drinks my potions or no. It will merely go harder with him if he does not have them. While away viking, he will have to go through this many times. So leave me to my work, that I might fortify him before he sails."

Eadha's stomach turned, but she kept her heart high. *If* he sailed, she thought. She possessed persuasions this old man did not, and might yet convince Tolljur round to her point of view.

169

Chapter Twenty-Two

"We are set to leave the day after the morrow. I began to think I would have to send men to drag you out of your hut—and away from that new wife of yours."

Gunnar sounded amused, but the gaze that raked Tolljur from head to foot remained sharp. He went on, "I only hope you can be prepared by the time we depart. Honeymooning can take a toll on a man."

Tolljur said nothing, but his heart twisted in his chest. The last—the very last thing he wanted—was to leave Eadha and set sail.

Apparently having no trouble judging Tolljur's expression, Gunnar grimaced. "I did warn you, Tolljur, you would not have time for a full honeymoon."

"*Ja*, Jarl Gunnar, so you did."

"You will be able to complete it when you return, with still more prestige and more wealth to heap upon your bride. She will forgive you then. And, long as you have been shut away together, you likely already have got her with child, *nei*?"

Tolljur devoutly hoped not.

Gunnar clapped him on the back and walked him to the door of the hall, from where they could see the harbor below. He indicated the longships, their carved dragon's heads rising high above the water. From here it looked like insects swarmed over them.

"Nearly loaded, as you can see," Gunnar said. "Friti and the others are eager to sail."

Tolljur grunted noncommittally. "Whence are we bound this voyage?"

"Back to Alba, of course." Gunnar grinned, revealing big square teeth, one of which was chipped. "Ours for the plucking, just like a virgin."

"Virgin no longer, surely. We cannot keep raiding the same settlements. We have already taken everything of worth, *ja*?"

"We shall try our luck on another island or another stretch of that coast. We are always successful in our strength. The gods smile on us."

"*Ja*." Tolljur turned from the scene below to stare into Gunnar's eyes. "One thing—if I go once more to lead your warriors in these raids, I would have your assurance my bride will be safe in my absence."

Gunnar looked surprised. "Why would she not be safe?"

"She is a stranger here, an outsider. There is some resentment because I have elevated her to the place of wife. I would not have her hounded or bothered while I am away."

"Tolljur, you know what the women of this settlement are. Might as well persuade ravens to be silent, as them. And they pick one another apart like ravens as well. She will have to find her own way. Me, I saw little weakness in her."

"There is little weakness," Tolljur agreed. He could not whine and express his concern over Eadha's possible unhappiness. His one comfort lay in the fact that Gunnar had already said Friti would accompany them away. At least Eadha need not fear his advances.

Laura Strickland

"Have you been to see Kaddi? No? Go now and fortify yourself. Time is short."

So it was—far too short. Tolljur wanted to spend it all buried inside his wife, feeling her, tasting her. But he nodded.

Day after next. He should already have taken several of Kaddi's potions.

Gunnar slapped his shoulder again in parting. "Women are but women," he said. "We live to go viking."

Tolljur walked from the jarl's hall up the hill, with the beautiful day dancing around him. Birds wheeled and cried overhead, and a stiff breeze blew inshore, striking sparks of brightness off the waves. He had nearly reached Kaddi's door when someone stepped out.

Two someones.

Eadha here? She broke off her conversation with the old man when she saw Tolljur.

And why should she come to Kaddi? Tolljur looked from her face to Kaddi's and back again. Neither told him much.

"Wife," he greeted her.

To his surprise she reached out immediately and clasped his hands. At the contact, some of the yawning emptiness inside him eased. But he asked, "What are you doing here?"

"I had questions for Master Kaddi. He has answered them as best he could."

"Questions?"

"About you." She added before he could press her farther, "Master Kaddi tells me the raiding party is to leave soon."

172

Was that devastation he saw in her eyes? Surely not. "Day after next." He confirmed starkly, and her mouth grew grim.

"That does not leave us much time."

He drew her closer. "*Nei*." He had felt the warmth of her passion these many nights and days. But dared he believe she would truly mourn his absence?

"Tolljur—"

"Hush. It will be all right. This is the way of our people, you understand. Men go and women stay. And you will not be alone. Kaddi remains, as does Inger and your friend Catrin."

"You would have me turn for solace to Inger?"

He wanted her to turn for solace to no one. Part of him deep inside wanted her to long for him, to miss him like a severed limb while he was away from her. The rest of him, though, wished to provide her what comfort he could.

He shook his head. "Wife, I cannot change this thing. It is as it has always been."

She nodded, bit her lip, and said, "At least come home with me now."

"I cannot. I must stay here with Kaddi and prepare. Already I have waited overlong."

"Then I will stay with you."

"*Nei*. There are things you should not see."

Her eyes widened in alarm. "What things?"

"Go home and air out the hut. I will come to you when I can."

For an instant he thought she would disobey; her defiance never lay far beneath the surface. Instead she stepped up and, right before Kaddi, gave him the kind of kiss that fired a man to his toes.

"See that you do."

She went off down the hill, and Kaddi raised his eyebrows at Tolljur. "Well, you have a handful there, it seems."

"Two hands full," Tolljur admitted, and smiled.

****

"Tell me about these scars on your cheeks," Eadha requested, and caressed them. "All the others on your body look like they were taken in battle—not these."

Through half-lidded eyes, Tolljur surveyed the room. The fire burned well and the floor had been swept. The bedding had been aired and new rushes scented the place. His wife had already loved him well—twice—licking every separate part of him before cuddling close and lifting her fingers to his face.

More than half bemused, he sought for words in his mind. He had never been with a woman directly after having taken one of Kaddi's potions. The drink heightened things, intensifying the experience almost unbearably.

Now he lifted a hand and very gently traced the mark on Eadha's cheek in turn. "Those were not taken in battle," he admitted. "They are my Marks."

"Marks?"

"I know no other word for it in your tongue. They are the claws of the bear, showing me to be Bearshirt."

"Oh." She seemed to contemplate that for a moment before she returned, "Marks of ownership, then."

"*Ja*—that."

She stretched up slowly and traced the deep furrows with her tongue, first one side and then the other. Into his ear she whispered, "But I hoped I owned

174

you."

What could he say to that? She owned his heart, but as yet they had refrained from speaking of love. Dared he, now?

The best he could do was give her the truth. "I belong to the gods before you, as does every man before his wife. This I cannot change."

She kissed him, and desire roared through him in a blazing wave, even though he'd just had her. She plundered the inside of his mouth deliberately with her tongue, reducing his bones to water.

"Not good enough," she whispered then. "I want all of you to belong to me."

Very gently, he caught her shoulders between his hands. "Eadha, listen to me. I can give you many things—the protection of my status and position, this dwelling away from others, where we have some measure of privacy. A hearth of your own over which you may play queen. Wealth. These things are earned by what I am—not given freely, you understand."

"I care about none of that."

"You must. Had I not been foremost among warriors, I could not have claimed you. You would have gone to another, probably Friti."

She went very still, and lowering his voice, he insisted, "It is the only reason you accepted me—to avoid that fate."

"Aye, but..." Earnestly she gazed into his eyes. "'Tis no' the reason I stay with you."

"Is it not?"

"Nay. Tolljur Magnussen, can you no' feel what is in my heart? If you can, then I beg you keep from going off with the others and attacking my people again."

"Your people?"

"How can I watch you sail away, knowing you go only to harm them?"

Tolljur went still in turn. So that *was* the true reason for all the kisses, warmth, and sweetness. Did she seduce, plead, and please only in an effort to turn him from harming those she truly did love?

His heart sank sickeningly. Very carefully he said, "You may rest your mind on that score, Eadha. We will not return to that same stretch of coast."

"Are you sure?"

"Sure—*ja*. Jarl Gunnar demands better. The wealth of your people has been exhausted."

She began to weep—in relief or sorrow, he could not tell which. He put her from him with gentle hands and tucked the blankets around her.

"Rest, wife. It has been a difficult day."

"Hold me, Tolljur, please."

He did so, his heart aching.

Chapter Twenty-Three

Sunlight bright enough to blind Eadha's eyes flooded in with Tolljur when he entered the dwelling. He stood for a moment while Eadha supposed he allowed his vision to adjust.

The ache in her chest, the same that always started when he left her presence, eased slightly. Och, how would she ever bear it when he sailed?

Tomorrow morning.

Aye, unless she yet persuaded him to stay. She'd tried already, so many times, and now had only the night ahead to work the miracle. Yet she sensed something between them had changed since yesterday. She blamed it on the potions Kaddi fed Tolljur. She turned now to face him, measuring his mood with her eyes.

"Welcome home, husband." Every impulse bade her go to him, to press her way into his arms. Something in his eyes, though, prevented it.

"Eadha," he said.

"I have prepared your supper and managed not to burn it too badly. Would you like to eat now? Or—after I welcome you properly?"

He moved at last, divested himself of the bear cloak, and approached the hearth.

"There is a feast in Gunnar's hall. I should attend."

Her heart fell violently. "But this is our last night

together!" She wailed it like a child. "My last chance, for who knows how long, to love you."

There, she had said it—the word with which she'd intended to gift him this night. Would he accept the gift or assume she spoke only of physical loving?

"It is a leave-taking celebration. You may come with me."

"And may I do this there?"

She approached him, cradled his face between her hands and stretched up on her toes to kiss him. He tasted of odd things, and she realized with shock the kiss must be flavored by Kaddi's potions.

After a moment, though, he began to participate enthusiastically. His arms closed around her, and he drew her nearer. His tongue caressed hers before setting up a steady rhythm.

She bit gently at his bottom lip and drew away far enough to gaze into his eyes. "Stay with me, Tolljur. I do not wish to spend what short time we ha' left among others."

"It is expected."

"Surely not. Will others not understand that with a honeymoon interrupted, you want every moment with your new wife?"

He did, did he not? Yet Eadha sensed a hesitation not present in him before.

"*Ja*, perhaps."

"Stay with me," she urged again. "I promise you will not regret it."

"Regret?" His lips twisted. "Regret and I are old companions." He captured her hand, which she'd trailed down his chest. "Wife, the potions Kaddi has given me are very strong. I am not at all certain I can satisfy you this night."

"Allow me to worry about that."

Now he caught her face between his hands and kissed her hungrily. "There are matters that must be discussed, Eadha. If I fail to return—"

"Hush. Do not say such a thing!"

"It is always a possibility. Or I may return on my shield. I have protected you as best I can. You will have all my wealth. A measure of influence. You could marry again, but if you do, choose him carefully—none of Friti's crowd, mind. Or you might buy your way free and go home." The crooked smile once more tugged at his mouth. "So you see, there is at least one good reason for you to hope I do not return."

"I will not listen to such words! Do you no' understand how I feel for you, Tolljur Magnussen?"

"I confess I have wished to hear that from your lips."

"It will tear my heart out to watch you board that ship tomorrow morning. And I shall be dancing on a knife's edge every moment you are gone."

"You speak truly, wife?"

"I speak truly, Tolljur."

He sighed, and something in him eased. The man she had known these many days once more looked at her from his eyes. "Then I will give the feast a miss and remain here with you—one last night."

"Aye, husband. And let us see if we can burn the memories deep enough to last."

****

Eadha slid her way up her husband's body and gazed deep into his eyes. Of all the things she loved about Tolljur Magnussen, all the things about him that pleased and pleasured her, she believed she loved his eyes best—clear as water, they made transparent portals to his soul. There she saw not the warrior, not the berserker, but the man.

How would she ever endure living without him? As ever when she thought on it, devastation hit her a staggering blow. Aye, well, the night had not ended; she had time yet to talk him round and keep him from going. Yet the potions he had taken did affect him, heightening some responses and slowing others. She made love to his body yet needed to reach his mind.

At this particular moment, sated, he lay like one half slain. In an effort to snag his attention, she breathed into his ear, "Well, husband, and do I please you?"

"Umm." He seemed capable of no more. Weakened? Defenseless? Eadha did not know. But she must speak now or not at all.

"Tolljur."

He focused on her more sharply, as if he could not help but answer her call. Their souls connected, and Eadha completely lost her thread of thought.

She loved this man—completely, impossibly. No matter where he went or what he became. *Oh, Lugh, oh, Lugh, help me. I love him and fear I will lose him.*

Heart aching within her, she breathed, "I wish to make another bargain with you."

"Bargain? We are man and wife. We need make no more bargains."

"I think you will like my terms. But listen."

"I listen." He lay and breathed gently, scarred chest rising and falling beneath her hands.

Her heart began to beat high and hard; she was about to spend the last of her ammunition. "Stay with me," she begged. "Do not go off on this raid."

"Eadha," he began. "I have told you—"

"Nay, but listen to the rest of it. Stay back from this voyage and I promise in return I will put aside my longing for home and remain here with you, joyful and obedient, all my life long."

It was the best she had to offer. She only hoped he comprehended the magnitude of the sacrifice: a permanent parting from her family. Never again to experience fragile mornings on the shore below her father's dun, nights spent speaking with Lugh, and the constant songs of the seabirds…

She loved it all.

She loved Tolljur more.

He did seem to comprehend; his eyes widened. "You would do this for my sake?"

"I would. I will."

He stroked her hair, tangling his fingers in the clinging waves while thoughts moved in his eyes.

"It is a beautiful offer, Eadha."

"Then you accept?"

"I wish I could. I would give much that I might. I cannot."

"But—"

"Hush. I have explained this. If I could choose, I would. I have not the ability to choose."

"You can, though! You already ha' wealth enough. I ask for little but your presence. Is your life not your own?"

"*Nei*, it is not. This thing you have failed to understand from the beginning; it is not."

Disappointment swamped her, horror and terror so bright she could barely breathe. She hid her face against his shoulder, denial rampant.

"I am sorry," he told her. "You have made a bad bargain—in our marriage, in me. You would have done better to accept someone else."

"No, not that. Anything but that." She clutched him harder, knowing at that moment she would trade her past, her future, even her peace of mind just to be with this man.

"Eadha, look at me."

She lifted her face, eyes swimming with tears.

"Berserker is what I am before anything else. This you must accept once and for all."

All words stolen, she said nothing.

Gazing into her eyes, he went on, "I will do everything in my power to come back to you. Wait for me?"

"Aye."

"Then this will be our bargain, the only one I can make. You will wait, and I will return. If anything can bring me safe home, it will be the promise of being with you."

She nodded, tears trickling down her face.

"Now if you would do one more thing to please me this night…"

"Anything."

"Play for me on your harp—play my peace, my comfort, my rest. Something for me to carry with me while away, when the madness has ridden me hard, when I need you most."

Without a word she arose, donned her robe, and went to her harp. Putting all her heart, skill, and love into it, she played until dawn.

Chapter Twenty-Four

"And so, do you carry his child?"

Eadha, her gaze fixed on the horizon, spun where she stood when the sharp query found her ear. She'd lingered long after the dragon ships left the harbor to sail north and east, while the other folk trickled away in ones and twos. Now she could no longer see the boats in the distance—just a shining path of light leading into the limitless sea.

How very much things changed, she marveled. She'd gone from dreading the sight of those same ships off her father's coast to pinning her hope on the merest glimpse.

Reluctantly, she directed her attention to the woman who had walked up beside her: Anaborg Helmsdottir. Eadha had not seen much of her—well, she'd seen little enough of anyone since being shut away with Tolljur.

Now she searched Anaborg's eyes, able to find no kindness or sympathy. Instead Anaborg raked Eadha from head to foot with a glance as sharp as a knife.

"It was supposed to be me," she said, "who bore the next berserker."

Eadha, aching with loss, said nothing. What did— or did not—pass between her and Tolljur remained theirs alone.

Anaborg needed no encouragement. She lifted her

chin, and her golden hair spilled down her back; in the clear morning light she looked almost impossibly beautiful.

"If you carry his child," she snapped, "I expect you will think you are something—bearer of the next warrior to lead this company. You, who are nothing but a dirty slave."

"Dirty?" Eadha made her own perusal of Anaborg and allowed her eyebrow to rise. "At least I lie with only one man, and he my husband. You lie with everyone else's."

An ugly flush rose from Anaborg's bosom—well on display—to stain her cheeks. "I am of Norse blood," she declared. "Daughter of heroes. Worthy to carry the next berserker."

"And you ha' had every man here," Eadha could not keep from sneering, "including Friti and his father. All but mine."

She made as if to push past, but Anaborg reached out and closed cruel fingers around her arm. "I would have had Tolljur Bearshirt last—and for good—were it not for you. Bearing the next berserker would have been my honor."

"Perhaps. Perhaps not. Take your hand from me." Eadha drew away.

"Oh, *ja*, it is an honor, make no mistake. One which you cannot appreciate. I do not know what he sees in you, with your queer-colored eyes and your marred, freckled skin. It cannot be your talent in the bed. No woman has more talent than I."

"What makes you think he wants other men's leavings?" Eadha retorted unwisely.

"Like you, with a husband back home?" Anaborg

leaned closer, staring into Eadha's eyes. "Curious, how you could marry Tolljur Magussen when you are already wed. Do you not miss him, this southern husband of yours? Do you fret for him?" Cruelty blossomed in her eyes. "Mayhap on this journey our warriors will strike him dead."

"Leave me alone."

"*Nei*, I think not. Tell me, how do you make peace with that, lying with two husbands? Do you hope Tolljur does not return home?"

"I hope no such thing."

"Should Tolljur die, you will be a slave again— used by every man of this settlement. I shall see to it."

Eadha lifted her chin. "I have no wish to be like you."

"Me, I am no slave." Anaborg swore, using a word unfamiliar to Eadha. "You had better watch your back, bitch. You could suffer a mishap and lose that babe yet."

With those words she swept past Eadha, head high, and climbed the path that led from the harbor.

"You have an enemy there."

Eadha turned her head to find Kaddi at her shoulder. The old man could move with absolute silence when he chose. Eadha wondered if he could also appear and disappear at will. He'd been at the site, clad in his raven cloak and speaking charms or blessings when the boats sailed away.

"I am surrounded by nothing but enemies," she told him.

He lifted ragged brows. "I am not your enemy. And you do not carry Tolljur's child."

"Eh?"

"I would know. I would sense if the next berserker were on its way."

"Must any child of his be a berserker?" Eadha asked him, as she had Tolljur.

"*Nei*. It could be a girl."

"But any boy—?"

"*Ja*, most likely. A privileged bloodline."

"You consider it a privilege?"

"If you do not, then you have no understanding of the folk among whom you have come to dwell."

"Come to dwell through no choice of my own."

"You mean to tell me that, given the choice, you would refuse to stay with him?"

Eadha could not claim it. She turned her face away.

Kaddi too pushed past her. "Do as Anaborg tells you and watch your back. Come to me if you need; I will help you." He paused to glare at her with his one remaining eye. "Like a daughter. Understand?"

Somewhat to her surprise, Eadha did.

****

Husavik proved a very different place with the men away. The atmosphere eased and rules governing the inhabitants—including slaves—with it. Old men met in groups at the harbor, telling tales of their own past voyages. Women emerged into the mild weather and moved everywhere, full of gossip. Children ran wild as hounds.

Freedom, or restlessness? Eadha asked herself but found no answer. She could barely stand to remain in the hut without Tolljur. The first night she lay awake sounding the strings of her connection to him, hoping her empathy—which worked so well on others—would afford her a glimpse of how he fared.

It did not, and her longing grew into an edginess that drove her from her hearth day after day to seek out others of the women who'd been captured with her, or to walk aimlessly on the slope high above the harbor, gazing out to sea.

Catrin found her there one afternoon when the string of days had already stretched long, and paused beside her in the sun.

"What are you doing, Eadha?" Catrin asked, blowing out a breath. Her cheeks glowed, flushed by the warmth of the day as well as the climb, and her bairn made a bulge at the front of her dress.

When Eadha did not answer, Catrin went on, "I thought you might come by again today. Aileen and Morag are already at the hall, and Aileen could use the company."

Poor Aileen. The warrior who'd claimed her only weeks ago had already traded her to another in payment of his debts—an older man who used her harshly. Eadha wished passionately she could rescue the girl— rescue them all from their hard fates. "Her master has not gone, though," Eadha pointed out. "He will soon come looking for her."

"Perhaps, although even he has eased his stance since the warriors sailed. She needs some hope, and you might give her that."

Eadha stared at her friend with empty eyes. "Me? Hope?" Suddenly she wanted to choke on the tangle of longing and desperation that filled her. What could she say to Aileen? What, after having given her heart to one of their conquerors?

Catrin eyed her frankly. "You ken fine they still look to you. You are the only bit of home left to them here. And they see you holding your head high. Think what you will, that means much."

"Aye," Eadha said softly. "I will come down when I can." She eyed Catrin again. "How grows your babe? When are you due?"

"Come autumn. I know not if this be lad or lass, but the child is a vigorous one. They breed strong, these men. You?" She switched her gaze to Eadha's belly. "Are you carrying?"

Eadha shook her head. "Too soon to tell," she lied, though her menses had already come. Could she explain to Catrin, forced to accommodate her master in the public setting of the hall, that Tolljur refused to give her a child?

Nay.

Curiously she asked, "What becomes of bairns born to slaves here? Lad or lass."

Catrin pressed her lips together. "I have gathered it depends much upon who fathers them and how he feels about them. If he has no other issue, he might raise them up, at least the lads. Lasses are slaves like their mothers, with little hope of raising themselves."

"Has your master, Harald, other issue?"

"Oh, aye—grown children from a past marriage. His daughter has a bairn of her own."

Eadha wondered how Catrin felt about that but did not quite dare ask.

"But you—the exception to the rule—are no slave," Catrin pointed out. "Your child will be born to wealth and privilege."

Eadha smiled wryly. "Yet you warned me not to get chosen by the berserker."

"I did not know you would wed with him. It is

188

unheard of. That is why you give the others hope."

"Hope," Eadha repeated again. Her gaze once more sought the far horizon. "Of what? The men go sailing off; we stay, never to see home again."

"Never," Catrin agreed and a sorrowful silence fell.

Catrin broke it at length to say, "I should warn you: there are those here who would bring you down from your new, elevated place."

"Anaborg," Eadha stated, and Catrin looked surprised.

"You knew? She goes about asking those from back home about you—who you were there, and what they know of your husband. She whispers of spells cast—implies you enchanted the berserker and so convinced him to wed wi' you. She will turn others against you if she can."

"Has anyone spoken of me being daughter to the chief?"

"Not yet, I think, but 'tis only a matter of time. She offers comforts in exchange for information—and they are few."

"How can she move against me, whatever she learns? I have Tolljur's protection."

Tolljur, warm in her bed, his hands coaxing and claiming her. Longing hit her like the flick of a flail.

"You had better hope so. If she convinces these folk their gods have turned against you, I doubt even the berserker's influence could save you—and him away."

"Their gods? What has that to do with aught?"

"Their gods, do you no' ken, are capricious and full of tricks. Just like them."

"Thank you for the warning." Eadha promised, "I

will take heed."

"See you do. You are the only one in any position to help the rest of us."

Chapter Twenty-Five

Eadha arrived at Kaddi's hut the next morning, anxious to ask him about the extent of Anaborg's influence, but she had barely passed through his door before agony exploded in her head. The intensity of it struck her dumb and drove her to her knees.

She gasped and stared at nothing, as a door abruptly opened in her mind. Terrible images and emotions poured through: the crash of weapons, the glint of sunlight on water, the red hue of blood. Pain, black anger, and enraged helplessness, all carried on a sweeping wave of power. There on the floor she cowered and covered her head with both arms.

Aye, and she had felt this horror before—back at the bath house the day Tolljur's temper slipped its chain and he slid into his berserker's rage. But he was not here with her now.

Realization hit her like a bath of cold water. Not here with her, no, but she could feel him yet, despite the distance of ocean that separated them.

Somewhere far to the southeast he had just fallen into his berserker's rage.

She trembled and shuddered, only vaguely aware that Kaddi called her name. "Eadha? What is it? What is wrong?" The old man seized her arms and hauled her to her feet. "What has befallen you?"

"Not me. Not me, Kaddi. Tolljur."

191

Kaddi stared into her face, his single eye wide with alarm. "Ah! What magic is this? And what has befallen him? He lives?"

"He lives," Eadha affirmed. She could feel all of it, the agony of the fit, the weight of rage tearing through him. She could almost feel his pulse pounding. Lips barely moving, she breathed, "He has entered battle."

"How can you know this?" Kaddi squeezed her arms roughly. "Tell me."

"We remain connected. I can feel him—"

She broke off abruptly, Tolljur's emotions overwhelming her. Dimly she felt Kaddi push her down onto a rug. He hurried away, only to return with a cup which he thrust into her hands. "Drink this."

Frantic, she tried to push it away. "One of your potions?"

"*Nei*. Mead."

Eadha drank, choked, and drank again. To her horror, the sensations—those same Tolljur now experienced—intensified.

She let the cup slip through her fingers as her eyes rolled back in her head.

Kaddi seized her again. One gnarled hand on either side of her face, he forced her to look at him.

"Listen to me. You are here in Husavik. Safe."

Eadha gasped, "He has been wounded."

"And will be again, many times. You do not wish to share this battle with him." Kaddi spoke a word, swift and harsh, and darkness arose in Eadha's vision. The word tasted of magic—she knew its flavor—and she possessed no more resistance to it than to Tolljur's madness. The darkness swallowed her whole.

****

192

She regained her senses in pieces—hearing first, tiny trickles of sound that wound their way into her ear. A click of crockery. The whisper of footsteps. A muttered half word.

Touch came next: she rubbed her fingers across a rough blanket. It felt as if she lay prone, half turned on her side but otherwise disoriented.

She opened her eyes, but the darkness persisted. Nay—there was a glimmer of light as from a fire beyond her sight. Over her head stretched dusty rafters. But where?

She lay very quietly and searched her mind—her heart and spirit—for Tolljur. He had disappeared as completely as if she had never shared his awareness.

Panic forced her up on the pallet, choking. "Tolljur! He is dead!"

"*Nei, nei.*"

Someone bustled up. Curiously, she knew him by his scent—another sense returned—herbs, smoke, and magic. Kaddi.

"He is not dead. I would know."

"He is gone from my mind."

"His berserker rage has eased, that is all. For now, it has eased."

Eadha turned her head and gazed into the old man's face. "For now?"

He waved an arm. "He is out there—somewhere—and will soon enter battle again."

Anger rose up inside Eadha, anger and grief. "Nay. I do not want to feel that ever again. I do not want him to feel it."

Kaddi lowered himself beside the place where Eadha lay. To her surprise, he folded her hand between both of his, which felt rough and dry.

"How often do you suffer this ability, girl, to feel what others feel?"

Eadha shook her head. "Much of the time." Should she tell him she had sued Lugh for magic and received this ability instead? A troublesome and useless gift. "But not—not like this."

"Can you feel me?" Kaddi demanded. "Can you tell what I am thinking?"

"Nay, not what you are thinking. What you are feeling, a bit. People's strong emotions just come rushing at me—fear, cruelty, lust."

"And," Kaddi persisted, "is that why you accepted Tolljur? Because you felt what he is inside?"

"Nay," Eadha said again. "Usually I cannot feel him, for some reason—only when he falls into a rage." Or into the throes of passion. "Then I seem to experience it with him. I did no' dream it would still happen once he went so far away from me."

Kaddi muttered something that sounded like a curse. "Best to let no one else know you can do this thing."

"Aye, but if it comes upon me unexpectedly…"

"Then you say you have fallen ill, some female complaint."

"Who would believe that?"

"I, for one; do women not go mad at the beck of the moon?"

Eadha smiled grimly.

Kaddi arose, stiff in the limbs, and shuffled off to bring her a second cup of mead. "Drink this and tell me of your life before your capture."

Eadha sipped cautiously, her thoughts flying.

Dared she trust Kaddi with that knowledge? Had he her best interest at heart?

"You put a spell on me," she said instead.

With a grunt, he regained his seat.

"When I fell into the echo of Tolljur's fit," she insisted, "you spoke a word; it was magic."

"And, girl, how should you know that? How recognize magic when you hear it?"

"There was a man back home, a man not unlike you. He worshipped other gods, but he carried the same kind of belief—and magic."

"Ah. And you studied with this man?"

"Aye."

"Is that not unusual among your people, for a female to pursue such a path? I am surprised it was allowed."

"He understood the depth of my longing." A longing to follow that ancient way and be what she was not. Yet the magic had not come to her—just this terrible propensity to sense others' emotions, and now the sharing of Tolljur's pain.

At the thought of him, her heart leaped. Where was he now? Whence, beyond the trackless waters, did he rest? How terrible were the wounds he had taken, and how could he endure that blazing darkness time after time?

Kaddi summoned her back to herself. "But you were wife, back at your home. Did your husband not object to you following this spiritual path?"

"Nay."

"Your father, did he mind?"

"Master Kaddi, I can feel you prodding at me. But the information you seek will do you no good."

"I ask not for myself but on behalf of Tolljur."

"It will do him no good either."

Kaddi grunted. "That is for me to decide. Tell me, girl, do you want to go back to your husband?"

Eadha hesitated. Truth, or lies? Which should she give him? "Nay."

"Is that not strange?"

She lowered her voice, even though they remained very much alone. "Master Kaddi, I was never wed; there is no husband back home. It was a tale intended to protect me."

"Tolljur knows this?"

"Tolljur knows."

"Well, then, I must consult with my gods. As should you."

"Consult with your gods, why?"

"Because Tolljur is their possession. And because I must learn whether you are meant to walk the spiritual path. If they say *ja*, then I must offer it back to you."

"I do not understand."

"*Ja,* girl, I think you do. Whatever else, you are not stupid. What are the names of your gods?"

Hesitantly, Eadha replied, "I follow Manannan and the Great Dagda, of course. Lugh—"

"Ha! I recognize none of those, but it does not matter. If the gods—yours and mine—say you need to study magic, I will give you that training."

"But...yours is not the path I sought."

He pushed his face forward into hers. "Let me tell you this, girl: there is one great force that turns this world, just as there is but one tune to which it dances. Call those we follow what you will: Odin, Freya, Loki, Thor... It is not the name that matters but hearing the song. You understand?"

"I do."

"Then speak to your gods, and I shall do the same."

****

Lugh?

Eadha spoke the name across the shining expanse of black-and-silver water, an invocation. She had come to the shore—so different from the one back home, yet so much the same—to be alone and consider Kaddi's bidding. Yet here the beauty of the night caused her to freeze, with but the one word on her lips.

In this place at this time of year, it never truly grew dark. Light merely faded from the water. But now a moon—nearly full—rose in the east and spread her skirts across a blackness deeper than that which surrounded her in the sky.

These were the nights and sights that had always drawn Eadha, even from childhood, and caused her to seek the spiritual path. This beauty had prompted her to abandon dreams of hearth, husband, and bairns for that ineffable *something* that translated, for her, into Lugh's presence.

Who would have thought she would find it here? It lent Kaddi's words more credence and made her willing to accept what he had said.

Was she still meant to follow her god even if led by one who spoke to other gods? What a curious man was Kaddi. She sensed true power in him and wisdom akin to old Neal's. But what sort of man put out his own eye, even in the pursuit of wisdom?

And would he expect such devotion from her also?

Devotion. For the first time in her life she felt it divided, within her heart, between Lugh and Tolljur.

Laura Strickland

Who would have imagined such feelings might be aroused by a mere mortal man?

And yet, could Tolljur be considered merely mortal? Which of these Norse gods touched him and so summoned his fits of strength and madness? Would that god, as well as Lugh, heed her now?

Quickly she bent her head and spoke to the pale darkness, not for herself but for he who now dominated her heart.

Help him. Uplift him. Protect and sustain him. Give him endurance to sustain his wounds. Bring him home safe to me. But until then—let him know my presence, wherever he may be.

She never knew which god heard and answered, be he Lugh, the Dagda, or he who went by the name Eadha had heard Tolljur speak: Odin. But the now-familiar voice whispered to her mind.

Believe.

Her spirit lifted over the water and flew.

Chapter Twenty-Six

"Drink this."

Tolljur obeyed the familiar command when the cup touched his lips, even though the voice did not belong to Kaddi this time. He felt he should know to whom the voice did belong—it seemed well enough known, yet the answer, like so much else, slipped away from him.

He knew only that he hurt, the pain a beast that tore at him from many places and worried his body like a hound did a bone. So fierce was the sting, he could not tell its source, wound from wound, and he struggled to remember the raid just past.

He failed. He retained only the usual blur of sounds and colors. He never felt pain during battle, only after, and he never recalled his opponents.

The taste of Kaddi's bitter restorative flowed over his tongue. The fog in his mind cleared slowly, and the pain sharpened. He became aware of other things: night had fallen, and he must be aboard the longship, for he could feel its gentle movement on the water.

Judging from the level of the pain, he must be badly hurt indeed.

He opened his eyes. Three figures crouched around him: Mikka, the warrior who, with Friti, so often entered battle just behind him, Tiff, the slave who often brought him Kaddi's potions, and Gunnar himself, all dimly seen in the half light of the gloaming.

As soon as Tolljur's eyes opened, Gunnar spoke. "Keep still. You are not in good shape." His voice, noncommittal, gave away little, and Tolljur wondered again about the extent of his injuries. From the feel of it, he might well have an arm off.

But, *nei*. He flexed his hands. The pain flared sickeningly, but his fingers obeyed.

Gunnar went on, "The battle did not go well."

"Eh?"

"They stood prepared for us—the men of several settlements together, it must have been. We did some damage, but they damaged us also."

"*Ja.*"

Dim images flooded Tolljur's mind: the flash of swords, the flare of fire, a rocky shore, and men with hard weapons and still harder eyes.

"You fought well," Gunnar told him. "First among us as always. And will again."

Tolljur swiveled his eyes until his gaze found Gunnar's.

"For we have not finished here," Gunnar assured him. "We strike again at dawn. Tell me my berserker will be ready."

Tolljur, lying in agony and with exhaustion weighing every limb, knew very well what he was expected to say.

Though he had no idea how many nor how extensive his injuries might be, or how long he might have until dawn, he knew his one reason for existing was to enter battle at the head of these men. If he led them only to Valhalla, so be it.

He nodded.

"Good man," Gunnar approved, and Tolljur heard

him walk away.

Mikka took his place. "The slaves bring the dressings and will treat you, if you wish. You, as always, are first to be attended."

All too aware no berserker should ever show concern for his wounds, or admit they hampered him, he grated through his agony, "How bad—?"

"Not one of us goes untouched. You, being at the front of us, took the worst blows. These southerners battled hard and did their best to bring you down. Your monstrous strength, though, kept you fighting."

He hesitated and seemed to view Tolljur's injuries with doubt. "You *will* be able to fight at dawn?"

Tolljur drew a breath that flexed knives in his chest. "*Ja.*"

"Good. And I, as ever, shall be at your shoulder."

Mikka departed then, leaving Tolljur in the darkness and at the hands of Tiff, who brought him the mug of bitter liquid. Slaves offered respectfully to bind his wounds, but he shook his head. He could feel Kaddi's draught at work inside, but it barely touched his pain. He heard the slaves whisper to each other about him, but his awareness faded in and out, in rhythm with the tide beneath the ship, only his heartbeat steady.

Pain roused him again some time later, and he lay wondering where he was and, even more terrifyingly, if he was dying. Did Odin's handmaidens wait to conduct him to the halls of Valhalla? Surely he had earned such a place through endurance alone. And yet, and yet…

He could not go, could not depart this world if it meant he would not see Eadha again, never feel her again in his arms. He could not abandon her in Husavik among strangers, enemies, those who had no call to defend her, prey to all who would come.

He had to live, and he had to rise again. Not for Gunnar or even the honor of the gods.

Not for himself.

For Eadha.

He had promised her he would return.

He could have wept then—he, a strong man, berserker—because he knew he had not the strength he needed. How would he return to her if he could not even rise?

"Tolljur, my husband."

The words came from nowhere and everywhere—from the darkness and the well of his pain, from his heart. *Ja*, and he must be dreaming or experiencing a vision. It took him that way sometimes when the pain became too great and he fell in and out of consciousness.

But *nei,* for he felt her hands upon him, and he would know that touch anywhere.

They fluttered over his wounds, which still bled, brushed his battered hands, and came to rest on his face.

"Tolljur, och, Tolljur, what have they done to you? You are sorely hurt."

"Dying."

"Nay. Listen to me. You have such strength—"

"Spent." He struggled to think on it. "How is it you are here with me?" Perhaps he had already died. Possibly for him Valhalla consisted of eternity spent in Eadha's arms.

Ja, then he would be well content.

"I am here with you only in spirit. My god brought me. If you have not enough strength, I will lend you mine."

"In spirit?" He had heard of such miracles and wonders of the gods, mostly from Kaddi. He opened his eyes.

She bent over him, her freckled face tense with concern in the half light and her hair hanging down. Her eyes met his, and he went breathless at what he saw there.

Nei, not love—it could not be love. He had not bargained for that when he claimed her and had not dared hope for it when they wed. Anyway, why would a woman such as she—vital, full of intelligence, passion, and all that magical music—love him? Surely he still dreamed.

"But I can see you," he whispered. "Feel your touch. Is it magic?"

"A kind of magic, aye. Tolljur, my husband, what has befallen you?" She could not hide her distress.

"First into battle. Hard battle." The words were all he could manage.

"And you taking the brunt of it. Do they not know you are but flesh and blood?"

"*Nei*, I am more. Berserker."

All at once she wept over him, invisible tears he nevertheless felt strike his skin. "At least now," she said angrily, "they will bring you home. How soon can I expect you?"

He drew another breath with difficulty. "We attack again at dawn."

"What! Nay, it is impossible. You cannot."

"I must. I will. I will drink Kaddi's draughts…"

"Nay."

"…and bring you a full share of riches. Those—

those will see you well-provided, perhaps buy your way home when I am…gone."

"Tolljur, Tolljur listen to me." Again she seized his face between her hands. "I do no' want wealth, even should it buy me influence or my way home."

"You said you longed for your home."

"I said I would stay with you, did I not? Tolljur Magnussen, if you do not return to me, I cannot go on breathing. Without the promise of you in my days, I care for naught. Without being able to kiss you—" She broke off and pressed her lips to his in a gesture of pure sweetness and bonding that breathed life into him. Life and strength. Gently, he curled his battered fingers around her wrists and anchored himself to her light.

He could have gone on so forever, just kissing her. But she removed her lips from his at last and said, "Promise once more you will come home to me."

Tolljur did not believe, at that moment, he could keep such a promise. Another raid loomed with the morning, and even a berserker's flesh could withstand only so much. Yet she desired it, and he could deny this woman nothing.

"I will," he promised, "if you promise to stay with me the rest of the night until…until I must…"

"I will." And she cuddled in tight, a presence that sounded the very depths of comfort, and steadied his world.

Chapter Twenty-Seven

The hall of the Norse warriors once more roared with sound. Eadha, standing just behind the place Tolljur occupied at the high table, felt as if she'd been caught in a nightmare—one that brought the past upon her again. The noise, the flaring light, and the emotions battering her all invoked far too clearly the night she'd first been dragged into this room.

She had no wish to be here, but Tolljur, newly returned home, had insisted on coming, and she could not bear staying behind at the hut while he attended the feast.

She wanted him never to leave her again.

He and the other warriors had arrived in Husavik just yesterday; she'd been afforded but one night with him, and that spent in attempting to soothe his agony. Indeed, part of their precious time together had been spent in Kaddi's company. The old man had come with his potions and bandages and labored over Tolljur, trying to work a miracle. But after Kaddi left, the only relief Tolljur could find came when Eadha played her harp long into the night.

Now anger burned in Eadha's heart, flaring like one of the torches that lighted this place. She directed a glare at Gunnar, whom she held responsible for Tolljur's condition. Aye, the jarl had his successful raid and his plunder. But how could he justify sending a warrior so sore hurt into the fray again and again?

Many of the other warriors also carried wounds, though none rivaled Tolljur's dire injuries. Despite that, the men appeared ready to celebrate, as some great victory. Uneasy, Eadha stepped closer and placed her hands on Tolljur's shoulders in a gesture of ownership; he twitched in response but otherwise sat like a man carved from stone, betraying no hint of his pain. Yet when she touched him, she fancied she caught a hint of his emotions—so deep had the connection between them now become.

Gunnar, once more on the dais, raised both hands, and the noise in the hall dampened a bit. The jarl spoke, and though Eadha could understand few of his words, she found she had no need. Boasting, posturing, self-congratulating. Was this all that came at her husband's great cost?

Before they left his hut to come here, he had asked her, "Are there any goods or riches you would like me to claim on your behalf?"

With a kiss to his lips she'd assured him, "I have all I desire." His mere presence following their cruel separation satisfied her needs.

"And, wife," he had pressed as they departed, "you promise not to lose your temper there among that company?" He knew how bitter she felt, on his behalf, over the fact that he had been put so to battle again and again. "I would have you save face."

That she understood; did not the men of her father's clan answer to similar rules of pride and conduct? The worst offense might be an insult or a slanderous implication. And since she in essence represented Tolljur's face here, she agreed. But it became more and more difficult to remain silent when Gunnar stopped speaking and the chattel was hauled in by a number of brawny, sweating slaves.

To her, the treasure did not appear like treasure—more like the household belongings of ordinary folk. She struggled to close her mind to it, thinking about later—later when Tolljur might at last lie in her arms. She did not need to make love to him, merely hold him and absorb the reassurance of his presence. That, to her, represented all.

Yet household goods were not the only things the warriors had brought back. When the captives were paraded in, Eadha felt it like a blow to the heart. Aye, and this she could not stand. For this time there were not only women among those captured but children as well.

As they were led in sobbing and weeping, Tolljur raised a hand and covered Eadha's fingers which yet rested on his shoulder. And his strength, so lent, allowed her to keep a rein on her ire.

She could not imagine anything worse than what she and her sisters had endured. But the plight of the children—or perhaps, Eadha corrected herself, they should more be called youths—was indeed worse. Lads of perhaps twelve to fourteen and a few lasses near the same age, they had their heads bowed, faces pinched white, and looked paralyzed with fear. Eadha's response came swift and visceral.

Someone's beloved children, paraded before this howling crew—what would happen to them? Surely the lasses were too young to be taken as bed slaves...

As if he sensed her emotions, Tolljur tightened his fingers on hers. In response, she dropped to her knees at his shoulder.

"Tolljur, nay!" No captives of this age had been taken in the raid that netted her, Eadha. Yet no one here behaved as if this were unusual.

"Hush," he bade her. "Some things you cannot change."

"I am thinking some things I should."

He turned his head and looked at her with his clear-water eyes, one of which now lay in a bed of swelled, purple flesh. "Wife, this is not the place. You promised."

So she had. And what was important to this man must be important to her. But she'd never until this moment realized what a warrior she was, deep in her heart. Now she wanted to leap up and fight even if her tongue made her only weapon.

She thought of the captives—slaves—of Husavik, women like the one who served in the bath house, forced to provide pleasure on demand to any of the men who came there. And she wondered if the lass now pinned by so many eyes at the center of the floor, who cringed and shook, might not have to endure a similar fate.

"Nay," she said to herself. And then, *Please, Lugh, help me. Help them.*

The level of noise in the hall dropped again. Gunnar once more began to speak and looked at Tolljur. Extolling the berserker's deeds in battle? Eadha could not tell, but it sounded that way. He spoke a question to Tolljur, perhaps asking him if he wished to claim a captive—first choice as so often being his.

Tolljur shook his head. His ashen hair slid over the bandages he wore on both shoulders, and Eadha picked up his emotions even more strongly.

The jarl then looked at Friti, who rose lazily to his feet and strolled out from his place to put a large finger beneath the captive's chin, so to examine her. His fellows hooted, and the lass, with nowhere to hide, trembled more violently.

The man's attitude, predatory and sexual in nature, made Eadha's decision for her. She leaned in closer to Tolljur's ear.

"Husband, I ha' changed my mind. I do want you to claim something on my behalf."

"Eh?" He looked startled.

"I wish for a serving lass to help me about the hut. That lass. *Her*."

Comprehension flooded his eyes. But he said, "Eadha, wife, she is as good as claimed."

"But you have first right, aye? You can exercise your right as foremost of the warriors by virtue of your valor."

He shot a look at the lass who, fair hair tangled, now swayed on her feet amid the laughter of her captors. "*Ja*, Eadha, but what good will it do, saving one?"

"'Twill keep her from falling into Friti's hands." She would use Tolljur's dislike of Friti as she must. "And anyway, what good did it do, saving me?"

Tolljur squeezed her hand and raised a preemptive arm. "Jarl Gunnar—I make first claim upon this captive." He spoke in Gaelic and appeared as emotionless as he had on the night he claimed Eadha; her mind again slammed her back to those moments full of terror and trepidation.

"Eh?" Gunnar looked startled in turn. He said

something in Norse that provoked bawdy laughter—perhaps questioning why Tolljur required the lass when he had a new bride.

Aye, so they did mean for her to land in someone's bed.

Gunnar made a gesture that ended the presumptive laughter and nodded at Tolljur. The next captive, a lad, was led in.

Eadha leaped to her feet and hurried forward, giving Friti a glare in passing. She caught the terrified lass's hand even as Friti spread his arms and backed away.

Lugh had just given her a purpose—one that must be lived out here in Husavik.

****

"She would ha' ended in someone's bed, you ken," Eadha breathed into her husband's ear some time later as they lay in the dark.

He did not immediately answer, and she closed her eyes for an instant, absorbing the warmth and the rightness of his body pressed against hers. The agony of longing that had possessed her all the days of his absence eased at last, and her heart seemed to steady beneath her breast.

Their new servant, who said her name was Meghan, slept the sleep of the exhausted in the far corner, the same place Eadha had occupied on her first night. She'd told Eadha she hailed from the island of Jura and was but twelve years old.

So Gunnar had not gone back to the spent well he and his warriors had made of Eadha's home. But it did not matter; Meghan was still Alban and hence one of Eadha's own people.

Tolljur stirred and ran his fingers through her hair, his touch at once comforting and arousing.

"Perhaps," he whispered, "Friti would have rejected her and she would have been taken to serve some good wife in her household."

"Some *other* good wife?" she teased.

He returned, "Are you a good wife?"

"You tell me. Was the floor swept when you returned?"

"I forgot to notice."

"Were the blankets aired?"

"*Ja*, I think so."

"Was the bread burned?"

"Only on the bottom." As if to emphasize the point, his warm palm traveled to Eadha's buttocks in a caress, his thoughts plain.

Eadha caught her breath. "Husband, surely you are too sore hurt…"

"Do not tell me that. While I was away, I lived on the thought of touching you, tasting you." He kissed her lips and tugged the bottom one gently between his teeth, feeding a fire that seemed to have simmered inside Eadha for days.

She adored this man, and she desired him. But she had seen the state of his wounds and would sacrifice far more than her own pleasure before causing him harm.

He whispered into her ear, "Do you not want me inside you, wife?"

"More than anything."

He laughed softly, not enough to disturb the child across the way. "You are intelligent and resourceful. I am sure you can think of a way to spare me and yet bring me my satisfaction."

"Ah, so you would have me use my imagination." He caught the back of her head and kissed her deeply, sweetly, his tongue plundering the depths of her mouth.

"Umm," she murmured in appreciation. "I must admit, your persuasion prompts no end of ideas."

"Then show me, wife."

"Aye so I will. You just lie there, Tolljur Magnussen—great berserker—and allow me to worship you as I longed to do each moment you were away. But no moving, mind—I would no' have you strain yourself."

This time the chuckle rumbled up from his bandaged chest. "Some parts move without my permission, when I am near you."

"So I see." She reached down and caressed him. "I shall have to reward this part by paying it particular attention."

"*Ja*, you will. But first—" He caught her face between his hands and kissed her again, a gesture filled with passion and devotion. "I love you, Eadha berserker's wife."

Wife of a berserker. Ah, Lugh, to what have you brought me?

To a man who possessed a heart wide enough and deep enough to contain her whole world...

"I love you, Tolljur Magnussen," she said, and proved it.

Chapter Twenty-Eight

"Just how great is your fortune?" Eadha asked idly as she entwined her fingers with Tolljur's in the dark.

He'd been home four days and healed steadily—remarkably—on a combination of Kaddi's potions and Eadha's gentle lovemaking. Aye so, perhaps it was not always gentle, but he thrived on it.

As did she.

The new member of their household, Meghan, thrived as well, progressing from timid and tearful to grateful for Eadha's kindness. Tolljur she still feared, remembering him from the raid on her home.

"I saw him attacking us," she had confided in a whisper to Eadha, her gray eyes full of dread. "Streaming blood he was, but naught any of our warriors did could stop him, for all that."

"He will not harm you," Eadha assured her.

Unlike some other men of Husavik.

Eadha had made what she hoped were discreet inquiries—mostly through Inger—as to what had befallen the remaining captives brought back from the last raid.

One had gone into Friti's home, also the chief's house. Did Friti and his father share the women kept there? Eadha had shuddered at the thought.

Now Tolljur drew away slightly in order to cast her a look, barely visible in the lingering glow from the dying fire.

"What sort of question is that, wife?"

"A practical one. I did, after all, accept you for practical reasons. 'Tis only my good fortune I fell so deep in love." She leaned up and kissed him.

"And mine," he agreed. "So why do you ask now?"

Distracted by the wild, tangy taste of him, Eadha nearly forgot. "Och, I ha' plans for your wealth."

"Plans?" She felt wariness stiffen his muscles. "Should these plans alarm me?"

Eadha thought about it. "Perhaps. I will need your help with some of them. But first tell me this: how does it work in your world? Are your goods and possessions mine as well?"

"I have bestowed all that I own upon you, including my heart."

"Well, then. How great is your fortune?"

He hesitated an instant before he said, "You would suppose Gunnar, as jarl, might be the wealthiest man in Husavik."

"Aye."

"You would be wrong. My father had great wealth when he died, and I have acquired more. Now tell me, wife: has your lust turned to greed?"

"My lust will never turn to anything else when I am near you. What do you do with this great wealth of yours? You live modestly enough."

"I have the finest of weapons."

"Of course."

"The amulet. And other jewels, put away."

"Aye?"

"What else do I need?"

"Another dwelling. A larger one."

"I will build that, if you like." He sounded entirely willing—but she had not told him the rest of it yet.

"It shall be up on the hillside," she prompted, "above Kaddi's, perhaps."

"This will make you happy?" He caressed her hair.

"To begin. We will need the room, you see."

"For why?" he sounded cautious. He thought she meant to ask for a bairn again.

So she did—but later.

"For my sisters. You are good at bargaining. 'Tis how you folk live, aye? By bargaining."

"In part. You wish to make another bargain with me?"

"Aye. Nay. I wish you to bargain for some of the slaves—those who are my countrywomen. I want a dwelling large enough to house them all until we can send them home."

He sat up slowly, his hair trailing down his back. Even in the dark she could see how he stared at her. "Eh?"

Ignoring his reaction, she hurried on. "Saving Meghan was a fine, braw thing. But it is not enough. Surely you see that. So many others live in horrible circumstances, in terror. The lass in the bath house, for one."

"Eadha, wife…"

"Nay, but listen. If you purchase her—and it must be that she will be for sale, as everything here is for sale—we can bring her out of that hard existence and let her live safe in our household."

"She is but one. You mean to save them all?"

"If I can. I believe 'tis why I was brought here, Tolljur. To save them."

Again he caressed her hair. "I hoped you had come to save me."

"That too. But, husband, I have long asked the god I follow to lead me. And he has brought me here, to this. Meghan was first; the lass in the bath house will be next."

"Why her?"

"Did you not see the look in her eyes?"

"*Nei*, I confess I did not look."

"Well, I did. 'Tis no way to live, being forced to accommodate all comers."

"She belongs to Friti."

"All the more reason."

Tolljur went very still.

Impulsively Eadha asked, "What is the source of the trouble between you? Is it mere rivalry?"

"*Nei*."

"Then what?"

"I do not wish to speak of it."

"I hoped there would be no secrets between us."

"It is no secret. Ask anyone—ask Inger. She will tell you."

"I am asking my husband."

He groaned. Following an intense pause, he said, "As I have told you, I was not the only child my mother bore my father. I had a sister once, named Gyda. In truth, my mother bore many other *kinder*—all boys and all stillborn. It is not given for there to be more than one berserker born into the same family at each generation."

"I see."

"You do not. My father was much away, and the loss of the other babes made my mother still fonder of Gyda and me. We grew up close, being barely a year apart. Gyda grew up...beautiful."

"How beautiful?"

"She would shame a summer morning." Tolljur's voice turned dreamy.

"What happened to her?"

The pause this time drew out so long Eadha feared he would speak no more.

"She took her own life."

"What?" Eadha sat up in the bed. Caught in memories, Tolljur ignored her.

"After my father died, I immediately went into training as next berserker, in Kaddi's hands and those of the older warriors who knew what to make of me. Ma—I told you how she fell apart after my father went to Valhalla. She could not live without him."

A fist squeezed Eadha's heart. She understood all too well how she would feel if she lost this man who lit her world.

"How does Friti come into it?"

"After *modir* followed *fadir* from this world, Gyda was left much on her own. She had friends, *ja*, but also there was Friti and his crew. Friti had long paid Gyda attention—unwelcome attention. Thrice did he ask her to accept him as husband; as many times as she refuse. She confided in me that he made her skin crawl."

An apt description, Eadha had to admit, even from a woman who did not possess the faculties of a sensitive. "What happened?"

"Friti refused to take *nei* for an answer. He pestered her still. I did not know this at the time—Gyda did not wish to place more of a burden on me, when she knew I already struggled with all I had to learn and accept. I figured it out only later and had no proof..."

His voice died away before he concluded. "Had I proof, I would have killed him, berserker rage or no."

"Did he force her?"

"*Ja*, I believe he caught her alone some time that last summer and pressed his suit too hard. All I knew then was her manner changed. She grew quiet and ceased laughing; her cheek turned pale. She refused food and did not sleep. I thought perhaps she suffered in missing *modir*. They were so very close."

Tolljur turned his gaze on Eadha. "I have no proof even yet of what Friti did. I merely know." He thumped his fist against his heart. "Here."

"You say she took her own life?"

"*Ja*. And I did not know. I missed even that. I came home—late—from a full day's training. Kaddi had been feeding me his preparations. I thought Gyda asleep in her bed; I spent the night there in the same hut. Come morning, she did not rise, and I smelled...*ja*, the smell of blood is familiar to any warrior. She lay across her bed but not sleeping; she had used our father's blade on herself."

Eadha went still with horror. Compassion rose in a staggering wave and she reached out to Tolljur and drew him close, hoping he could feel her love.

He buried his face in her neck but did not weep, even though tears burned the back of Eadha's throat.

Through them she asked, "What made you suspect Friti, after?"

"His manner was not right. He did not behave like a man regretting the death of a woman he had long admired. And Gyda's friend came to me, told me what she suspected had happened between them. Not long after Gyda's funeral, I overheard Friti with his companions laughing—*laughing*—that at least someone had the pleasure of plucking Gyda before she went to her death.

"I challenged him on it. I stepped out and asked what he meant by those words, with the rage nibbling hard at me. He said only that my sister may not have been as pure as I'd believed."

"What did you then?"

"Somehow I kept from killing him where he stood. I went to Kaddi with the matter. He said men's talk was nothing I could take to Gunnar, and if I slew Friti without proof of his wrongdoing, I would be banished."

"Banished?" Kaddi had mentioned this before.

"*Ja*, at loose in the world with nowhere to lay my head. I have thought since—a thousand times—I should have treated Friti as he deserved and accepted the consequences. Life has not been so good in Husavik after all. But then," again he ran his fingers through Eadha's hair, "I never would have met you."

Eadha seized his hand and kissed the palm.

Bitterly, Tolljur went on, "I still have no proof—only what I feel in my heart."

"Listen to me, Tolljur: I believe what you suspect of Friti. I ha' felt what lies within that man, and 'tis dark and cruel—cruel enough to do such a deed and laugh about it."

Tolljur grimaced. "It was my fault as much as Friti's. I should have protected her from him. Failing that, I should have made him pay."

"You can, still."

"How?"

"By thwarting him whenever you get the chance. Do you no' see? He thinks he can have the world and every woman in it. He would have had Meghan. You are the only man here who has the means and the will to stop him. Can you not honor Gyda by saving these other women from her fate?"

Tolljur blinked at her, and a new look came into his eyes, part gratitude and part determination. "*Ja*, wife. Perhaps your god and mine can work together in this thing. Tell me again of your scheme."

Chapter Twenty-Nine

"You are greedy as well as ignorant. What is this, slave woman? Do you mean to bleed Tolljur Magnussen dry?"

Eadha spun as Anaborg's voice floated across the building site where she and Meghan worked in the afternoon sun, gathering stones. Anaborg possessed only a poor command of Eadha's tongue, but the expression in her eyes needed little interpretation. One searching glance told Eadha that Anaborg appeared both waspish and impatient, ready to cause trouble if she could.

She also looked as if she'd just come from someone's bed, hair tangled and lips swollen. Eadha wondered whom she had accommodated, and then decided she did not care.

Not waiting for an answer, Anaborg demanded, "Where is he?"

Eadha deliberately widened her eyes even as Meghan, staring curiously, shrank toward her side. "Where is whom?"

Anaborg's lush mouth curled in derision. "Tolljur Magnussen, fool."

"Ah, you speak of my husband. I am surprised you did not pass him on your way up."

Anaborg glanced down the slope as if searching for the one man among many, and Eadha wondered, not for the first time, about the nature of her true feelings for Tolljur. Oh, aye, when they were together Eadha sensed desire from her. Were there also more tender emotions?

She decided she did not care about that either.

"Where has he gone?" Anaborg demanded.

"What is it to you?"

In truth, Tolljur had gone to speak with Gunnar about procuring Brida, the girl from the bath house. This new dwelling would not be ready for some time, perhaps not until winter, but her situation haunted Eadha, and she'd begged him to act now.

"She will just be replaced by some other woman," Tolljur told her starkly as he departed. And that thought haunted Eadha as well.

How could she change things here for good and all? *Help me, Lugh*, she prayed yet again, and a seabird flew overhead, crying.

"You do not listen to me," Anaborg complained and raked Eadha with a hard look. "I still do not know what he sees in you—a slave, and ugly at that."

Meghan, still at Eadha's shoulder, made a soft sound of protest. She had at last stopped weeping for home and followed Eadha like a shadow.

"True," Eadha agreed dryly, "I am no' so beautiful as you."

Anaborg lifted her head arrogantly. "No one is as beautiful as me."

"Except Tolljur's sister, perhaps—Gyda. Did you know her well?"

Caution flooded Anaborg's eyes. "I had nothing to do with that."

"With what?"

"Her death, which was unfortunate. But we speak

of Tolljur and how you persuade him to build a palace that should have been mine."

"I do not make Tolljur Magnussen's choices for him, not where he builds or wi' whom he lies. Had he wanted you, he would ha' chosen you long before I came."

Anaborg's eyes flooded with consternation and spite. "*Ja*, well enjoy your place while you have it, slave. Many terrible things might happen to you: a fall on this steep path in the dark, a knifing, even a fire."

"Do you threaten me?"

"*Nei*, I say only that should some such thing happen to you, you would not be missed."

Not awaiting an answer from Eadha, Anaborg swept around and picked her way down the rocky slope. Eadha fought an impulse to plant both palms in the woman's back and push; she would not lower herself so far, though she acknowledged the desire.

"*Dhe*," Meghan breathed. "She means you ill."

Aye, Eadha thought, and Anaborg knew something, also, about Gyda's death.

Horrified, Meghan went on, "Nothing will happen to you, will it, Mistress Eadha? Who would protect me then?"

Eadha took the girl's hand. "Naught will befall me. Look—yon comes Master Tolljur."

Her heart lifted involuntarily at the sight of him, even as he and Anaborg paused in the act of passing each other, just above Kaddi's hut. They exchanged words, and Tolljur shook his head repeatedly before giving Anaborg his shoulder and coming on. Anaborg stood watching him for several moments as he climbed.

Eadha met Tolljur with an inquiring look even as

Meghan melted away some distance. Still uncomfortable with Tolljur, she kept away from him when she could.

"You did not bring the lass, Brida?"

He shook his head with regret. "Jarl Gunnar refuses to negotiate over her with me. He claims she belongs to Friti and I must deal with him. Friti will keep her just to thwart me." He eyed Eadha unhappily. "I told you, wife, you cannot save them all."

True—Eadha could not save Catrin either, nor, she feared, any of the lasses brought here with her from Alba. Tolljur said Catrin's master, Harald, would never part with her so long as she carried his child. The other Norse men who had claimed women considered them property too valuable to part with readily. Eadha, feeling frustrated, turned her eyes on the scene below. "Where is he now, that Friti?"

"At the harbor, overseeing the preparation of the longships."

That drew her gaze back to his face; a gasp escaped her lips. "Nay, not so soon. You are no' ready to go back raiding."

He shrugged ruefully. "The season for viking is short, and we need all the wealth I can procure to carry out your plans."

"Nay," she said again and seized his arm. "You have had no time to recover." Dread made her suddenly breathless. "You are not fit to fight."

"I must become fit. I am berserker. Battle is my reason to exist."

"Nay; loving me is your reason. And what we are to accomplish—together."

"What is that, wife?"

"A new world, a better one where, as you said, your god and mine live in harmony."

"It is a good dream."

"More than that, Tolljur. I am determined on it. What would happen if you refused to accompany the others on this voyage?"

He frowned. "I am not at all sure they would agree to go without me."

"Then let them wait until you are fully recovered. Let them wait forever."

And, putting her whole heart into it, she kissed him.

****

Tolljur ducked beneath the lintel of the bath house and blinked at the scene within. Some eight warriors occupied the place amid clouds of steam—Friti and his usual band of cronies. They looked up when Tolljur entered, displaying varying measures of respect—all but Friti, whose expression remained lofty, and one other man, fully distracted by a woman who tended him, in the far corner.

Tolljur looked round in an effort to locate the slave about whom his wife expressed such concern. Dismayed, he recognized her as the young woman engaged with the man who'd ignored Tolljur's arrival—with good reason.

Tolljur's resolve hardened. He did not know but what Odin had sent Eadha to him, with her fierce heart and her determination to change things. But *ja*, in this instance, much needed to change.

"Ah," Friti decried lazily, "it is our esteemed Bearshirt. But what is this I hear of you, Tolljur Magnussen? You have told my father you will not sail with us on our next voyage."

The other men exclaimed with genuine protest. Tolljur represented their security in battle. So used were they to following his back into every fray, as they might a standard, they likely could not imagine a battle devoid of his presence.

Calmly he said, "*Ja*—I am slow to recover from my last injuries."

"Slow to recover?" Friti repeated it with patent disbelief. "But you are berserker, able to recover from any injury. You are reluctant to leave that new wife of yours, I think you mean. I suspect she is a witch and has cast a spell on you."

The other men went suddenly quiet. It did not do to speak of dark enchantments, or those who cast them.

Tolljur smiled grimly. "If you believe me enchanted, Friti, you will not want me aboard the ship for fear I may make it founder."

Friti's gaze turned cold. "We take chances every day, and the season for acquiring wealth is short. I should think you would be eager for more riches, given what you are planning upon the hill." Friti paused and added with weight, "You should take care with that. My father will not like it if you outshine his hall."

"*Ja*? And what will he do then?"

"He may declare that wife of yours bad luck and banish her."

"If she goes," Tolljur stated quietly, "I go with her."

The men all stared, including the one from whose feet the slave girl now arose. She moved to stand by the wall and Tolljur caught a glimpse of the look in her eyes.

Anger flooded his heart.

"Fool," Friti decried. "The world is full of willing women." He gestured roughly at the slave.

Ja, Tolljur thought, and some not so willing. Did Friti even remember Gyda, whose life he had destroyed? The anger within him quickened and threatened to become rage, but he beat it back and lifted his head.

"I am foremost of Jarl Gunnar's warriors." Uncontestable. "I sail if and when I choose."

For the first time, consternation showed in Friti's face. The others stirred uneasily and exchanged glances.

"*Ja*, well, Tolljur, perhaps the voyage can be delayed a few days until you deem yourself ready."

"I may not be ready until spring," Tolljur said flatly. "Meanwhile I would discuss a matter with you, Friti. Step outside with me."

Friti, loath to accept commands, rose languidly and followed Tolljur from the bath house, naked as he stood. They faced one another in the late afternoon sunshine.

"What is it, berserker?"

"I wish to make you an offer for one of your slaves."

"Eh?" Friti's blue eyes narrowed in surprise. "But you just acquired a new slave at the last feast."

"I want the girl within."

"What?"

Tolljur jerked his head. "From the bath house."

"Why? Does your wife not provide you enough pleasure?"

Tolljur stood like stone.

"*Nei*," Friti said then. "We have just got her trained up proper. Teaching another would take time."

Just as he had told Eadha, Tolljur reflected. Saving one girl would only put another at risk. Yet he remembered the look in the slave's eyes and did not waver.

"Name your price."

Uncertainly moved in Friti's gaze, followed by cunning. "She has no price, berserker."

Tolljur echoed Eadha. "Everything has a price."

"Including your service?" Friti stepped up closer. "I want this voyage, Tolljur. And I want you on it. I will exchange the girl inside for that—no more, no less."

Dismay struck Tolljur in the gut, hard. He knew his body unready for battle, and he did not want to leave Eadha so soon. By Odin's eye, he did not want to leave her at all. But he knew Friti for a hard bargainer. And he had glimpsed Gyda in the eyes of the girl in the bath house.

"Delay the voyage a sevennight, and I will accompany you," he granted. "But I take the slave now—today."

"She is not done with her tasks inside."

"She will have to be done."

Friti's eyes narrowed.

"What is it, Friti Gunnarssen?" Tolljur challenged. "Do you not trust my word?" He leaned closer and bared his teeth. "Believe me: when I vow something, I fulfill it." Like long-overdue revenge.

Friti jerked his head at the doorway. "Then take her, Tolljur Magnussen."

Chapter Thirty

"I did not ask you to trade your safety for hers! Why would you make such a reckless agreement? You are not fit to sail."

Tolljur had never before seen his wife in a rage. To be sure, he had rarely beheld such anger from anyone, berserkers aside. He had expected her to be displeased with his bargain but thought the presence of the slave, Brida, might go far toward placating her.

Not so. Now he stood beside his own hearth as at the middle of a maelstrom while his possessions flew around him and the two slaves huddled together in the far corner. His wife threw things when angry—and with deadly accuracy.

He found it encouraging that she had not yet hit him; she could if she wished. Not completely out of control, then.

"How could you risk yourself so?" A jug of mead smashed on the hearth beside him. "You ken fine you are no' ready to fight." Two bowls and a cup hit the wall behind him.

"You wanted the girl's freedom," he put in.

"Not at the cost of your life! How can we help anyone then? How can I go on if I lose you?"

She seized her harp, the only thing left to hand, and prepared to heave it. In two strides he stepped forward and caught her.

"*Nei*, you shall not."

Instantly she collapsed into his arms, the rage draining from her as abruptly as it had come. He felt devastation replace it, and she dissolved into tears, sagging against him.

"I cannot hope to live without you, Tolljur. The very thought terrifies me."

"Hush, hush." Disregarding the women, he set the harp aside, caught her up, and carried her to their bed. "List. List to me." Putting her down softly, he brushed the hair from her eyes and only half saw Meghan and Brida tiptoe from the hut.

"I will return to you. We are not so easy to kill, berserkers. Remember, blade cannot fell us in battle, nor flame."

She gulped back her tears and glared at him. "Do you take me for a fool?"

"Anything but that." Did he not love her quick mind as much as her soft flesh?

"Swords and flames cannot *halt* you in battle—I know you barely feel them whilst caught in the berserker's rage. That does not mean they do no' harm you." Frantically, her hands raced over him. "I have seen—and felt—their effects."

"*Ja.*" That he could not deny.

"And your father—he may not have died in a battle, but he perished as a result of one."

Tolljur hesitated. He did not like thinking about his father, or the agonizing death he'd suffered after returning home.

Gravely he told her, "Out of spite, Friti would agree to make no other deal with me. And you were right. The girl needed to be freed from that place." He caressed her hair. "You, wife, are like the voice in my head telling me what is right, like one of Odin's ravens sitting on my shoulder."

"Then I tell you, Tolljur Magnussen—you must not go to fight. I feel the danger of it, here." She touched her breast.

"I vow to you, wife—" he cupped her face between his hands, "this will be the last time."

"Truly?" Her gaze brightened.

"Truly. When I return, I will put away my weapons, make best use of the wealth I have in store, and begin a new life with you."

Joy flooded her eyes, and he bent to kiss her, letting the sweetness of her claim him once again.

"And," he told her then, "do you not harm a string of that harp. I shall live on the promise of hearing you play it when I return."

"And on this," she added before pulling his head down again.

****

"Do not fuss and fly about him so, woman," Kaddi chastened Eadha sternly. "Allow the man some dignity."

Eadha, eyes fixed on Tolljur's face as he stepped away from her and boarded the longship, ignored Kaddi's scolding. Already a small span of water separated her from Tolljur, and she felt it like a physical pain. How would she ever bear it when that water widened and the boat sailed from the bay?

Tolljur looked impassive, giving no hint of his emotions. Yet she could feel her own tension reflected in him, just as she could feel the wounds he bore beneath his leather armor.

Despite those wounds, they'd made frenzied and desperate love last night while the two slaves slept. And this morning she had said over him every charm of which she could conceive.

It might not be enough.

Beneath her breath she muttered, "What if I never see him again?"

Kaddi turned on her. "Do not speak such words! Do you not know giving voice to your fears may make them come true? Trust in your gods—and mine."

Aye so, the old man was right. Yet the feeling of malaise that gripped Eadha refused to lessen.

"Had he sufficient preparation?" she questioned. "Did those vile potions of yours have time enough to work?"

"He has taken more with him. Come, girl, you have much to do at the building site while he is away, and it is bad luck to watch the boat out of sight."

But Eadha did not stir, her gaze still fixed on her husband. She heard again the words he'd tumbled into her ear just before boarding the deep-water vessel.

I love you. And I will return.

See you do, she told him now, spirit to spirit. *For you carry with you my heart.*

The onlookers left the harbor one by one, but Eadha remained in defiance of Kaddi's warning until Tolljur's ship disappeared into the white haze of the horizon. Then she drew a breath, wondering how she was to exist until it sailed back again.

Protect him, Lugh.

Strange how the god had worked in her. She had spent most her life seeking Lugh's company and wisdom, a pursuit she'd believed interrupted by the cruel raids that destroyed her cherished existence. But aye, Lugh had used those raids to bring her to this place and a love she could never have imagined, a cause far more important than her own desires.

Kaddi spoke true. She had much work ahead.

She turned from the harbor at last and started, finding Anaborg directly behind her. The woman's gaze narrowed sharply and a cruel smile curled her lips.

"I suppose you would like me to believe that now you will pine for him." Anaborg's eyes raked Eadha up and down. "Your enchantments may work on him—a man—but mean nothing to me."

Eadha tried to push past the other woman. "Leave me be, Anaborg Helmsdottir."

"*Ja,* so I will." Anaborg's eyes flooded with spite. "Just so long as you remember it is dangerous to walk here on the rocks or up on the hill without Tolljur to protect you."

Eadha turned. "That, again?"

"Forgive me expressing my…concern. As I told you before, many things may happen to a woman who is alone in the dark—a fall, a blow." Anaborg leaned closer. "When he returns, he will be mine—and that grand hall with him."

****

A shiver traveled down Tolljur's back, as if some ill spirit trod his spine with cold feet. He stood still at the side of the ship even as the sail fluttered above him, seeking a last glimpse of the bay at Husavik, and Eadha with it. He could no longer see her, and he sent a prayer to Odin even as he searched his heart.

Ja—she remained there still, the most precious of all that he held dear, this woman he had claimed on a whim and who now gave meaning to his days. How long he had waited for her, blind and aching. And now but one more voyage separated him and a new life.

Someone leaned on the oaken gunwale beside him. Friti hung his shield on the side of the ship before directing a look at Tolljur.

"So, berserker, and do you now find yourself fit for battle?"

A good question, but the barely covert gloating Tolljur heard in Friti's voice bade him answer in the affirmative.

"*Ja*, sure."

"Only you seemed unusually reluctant to undertake this journey. Perhaps you were just loath, after all, to leave that new wife."

Tolljur said nothing, and Friti mused on. "A man wishes to be at his best entering battle. And his mind must be at ease also. I would hate for you to doubt your strength—for the first time ever—or worry about the safety of your wife while you are away."

Tolljur turned his head and stared into Friti's eyes. "Are you saying I need to worry about her?" His uneasiness on that score, always close to the surface, promptly reared its head. He told himself, not for the first time, that Eadha had the protection of their gods, and Kaddi remained near at hand.

Friti gave an elaborate shrug, playing at carelessness. "Of course not. But one never knows; life is a dangerous gamble. Wives—as well as slaves—have been known to suffer mishaps while their men are off viking."

Disquiet, still more fierce and deep, stirred in Tolljur's heart. "Explain yourself."

Friti, however, merely lifted his brows and changed the topic. "How long have we known each other, Tolljur Magnussen?"

"All our lives."

"All our lives, *ja*—we grew up together. And, always with a rivalry between us, *nei*? Were you not berserker, I would be first among our warriors in every battle, the best spoils mine to claim. Including that new wife of yours to use and toss aside."

"So?" Tolljur returned angrily.

"So it occurs to me," aggression sparkled in Friti's blue eyes, "should something dire happen to you in battle—because your mind was not at rest over the safety of your wife, perhaps—I could claim that first place still."

Friti unpropped himself from the rail and moved off, leaving Tolljur staring at the impossible gap of water between him and the most precious possession of his heart.

Chapter Thirty-One

Eadha paused in her place high above the settlement where she labored piling stones, and gazed out over the water. It had become a habit with her ever since Tolljur sailed away, a spiritual touchstone, assuring her he had only to sail back into that bay once more in order for her to feel complete. By Lugh's shining spear, how she missed him! His absence felt like a raw wound in her heart. So far, she'd filled up the days as best she could, working here on the building site, striving to make Brida and Meghan comfortable and secure in Tolljur's household, and visiting with Catrin and others of her fellow clanswomen as often as she could. She would like nothing better than to get Catrin out of Harald's possession, but it was as Tolljur said; the jarl's man was not likely to part with any woman carrying his child.

Determination strengthened Eadha's resolve. She intended to improve the lot of as many of her countrywomen as she could. There in the warm sunshine, she marveled once again at how Lugh had brought her to this sacred obligation.

Just below her on the site, Meghan and Brida chattered together in their own tongue, making Eadha smile. Mere days ago, Brida had refused to speak at all; now her voice floated on the morning air like that of a small bird, putting Eadha in mind of the times back home when the women had all worked on the shore together. Was there, after all, a possibility for them to heal and find a measure of happiness?

She moved higher up the slope and began humming to herself, one of the harp tunes Tolljur liked best. When next she straightened, the sun—slanting from the west—glinted off the water below, half-blinding her. As simply as that, she found herself caught as a wave of horror overtook her. The rocks she carried in her apron fell at her feet, and those who worked beside her—craftsmen and slaves alike—turned to stare.

"Mistress Eadha?" Meghan called, even as Eadha fell to her knees. The girl abandoned her own task and rushed to Eadha's side, where she hunkered down, her eyes wide with concern. "What is it?"

"Tolljur." Eadha could manage but the one word. Somewhere in the world—and she knew not where—he had fallen into his berserker's rage; she now felt his emotions as if they were her own.

"What of him?" Meghan seized Eadha's arms. "He is away on that dragon boat, is he not?"

"Entering battle. In danger." Eadha's eyes rolled back in her head. Before she lost consciousness, she heard Meghan scream to Brida, "Go—fetch Master Kaddi, quick as you can."

****

"Drink this." The voice belonged to Kaddi, as did the warm palm on Eadha's brow.

Eadha turned her face away. "Nay, I want none of your potions."

Kaddi chuckled. "You are returned to yourself, then."

A strange way to put it—returned to herself. But maybe not so strange, for she had piggybacked on Tolljur's spirit as he fell into his berserker's rage, only to lose track of him again now that the madness had passed.

Where was she? Struggling to sit up, she saw she lay in her own bed in Tolljur's hut. A fire burned low, and darkness filtered through the smoke hole. Brida and Meghan worked at the hearth, side by side.

Eadha eased back down.

In a low voice, Kaddi said, "You frightened your servants. The girl who came for me said you fell into a fit. But it was not a fit, was it? You have journeyed to Tolljur once again."

Eadha studied Kaddi's lined face with its puckered eye socket. She saw no need to try to spare the old man.

"Tolljur called me to him," she whispered, "from the throes of his berserker's rage. Indeed, it matters not how far away from me he is; I can feel his emotions, the darkness and pain that grip him."

Kaddi mumbled a word in his own tongue and made a quick gesture with his fingers. "It is a dire magic, and a true gift of the gods."

"If the gods mean it as a gift, then why is it I canna feel him until the rage takes him?"

Kaddi appeared to ponder that before giving a decisive nod. "It is the only time he lets go the fierce hold he keeps on himself. Can you feel if he is badly wounded?"

"I can, and he is. You and I know, Master Kaddi, he went into this voyage no' yet healed from his last injuries. I fear for him."

Kaddi closed his fingers on hers. "Let me tell you

something, girl. I love that young man like my own son. This eye I lost? It was given in service to his father, and to him. The wisdom I received in return I did not at that time understand. Odin told me a wave would one day come from the south—a silver wave that would lift Tolljur Bearshirt from his place among us and carry him to a new beginning." Kaddi smiled ruefully. "I did not guess that wave would be a woman."

"Me?" Eadha faltered.

"You have strength and purpose. You can lead him to this new life." Kaddi leaned closer, and his single, faded eye met Eadha's. In that instant she wondered if she spoke to Kaddi at all, or to some other being.

"But have a care for your safety," he cautioned her. "For you carry his heart, his sanity, and his life."

****

"Drink this."

Out of the darkness and fathomless well of pain, Tolljur felt the rim of a cup press to his lips. Whose voice was that? Not the one he'd expected.

With a staggering effort, he opened his eyes. He once more lay on the deck of the longship—he could tell that much by the movements of the vessel beneath him, well known as his own breath—and a thousand stars stretched overhead. It looked as if the gods had leaned down from Asgard and unfurled a jeweled cloak of night.

"Where is Tiff?" he asked.

The form directly above him shifted. "Killed in the fighting."

Grief squeezed Tolljur's heart, which seemed otherwise far too empty of emotion. The man—trained by Kaddi long ago—had served him well, voyage after voyage.

"Gunnar?" he asked next.

"Getting his wounds tended. Just drink."

Tolljur frowned. No one besides Tiff knew which of Kaddi's draughts to administer and when. He needed the restorative, and badly—he knew himself injured in a dire way, but tried to reach past that for memory.

"The fight did not go well." His mind groped through the scattered images.

A second shadow shifted against the jeweled sky, and a man hunkered down beside him. Gunnar. He answered, "It did not. The shore, here, runs red with our blood, but the gods have not completely forsaken us. Come the dawn, we will fight again and prove victorious."

"Drink your draught, Tolljur Magnussen."

Tolljur, still struggling to recall the battle just past, could remember only glimpses—fierce men in green tartan with flying hair and well-edged weapons. The rage that carried him through them with the helmeted company at his back. Blow upon blow rending his flesh, none of which he felt—until now.

For one bleak moment, facing the truth of that pain, he wanted to die. How easy it would be to surrender to the overwhelming weakness and stride into the hall at Valhalla. He would meet his father there, and perhaps Tiff as well.

If he stepped through the doors of Valhalla, though, he could not return to Eadha. The very thought of her lifted him above the pain, the way the tunes she played on her harp lifted him from his misery. Fey, clever woman with so much strength...his, his, *his*. *Nei*, and he could not go into death, for he had promised

Eadha—and himself—he would return to her.

A sound escaped him, half sigh and half groan. If he wished to return to her, it meant he had to face tomorrow's battle carrying these wounds that bit at him—face battle and survive.

"Drink," said the first man again, and tipped the cup so the liquid it held flowed past Tolljur's lips.

Not the restorative. Tolljur knew the taste of that—sharp, bitter, all too familiar. This substance tasted oily and noisome like nothing else that had ever before scorched his throat.

The man who had administered it leaned closer, and just like that Tolljur knew him by the hard gleam in his eyes and his sharp smile.

"There now, that will mend everything."

Friti. And what mischief of Loki's making had left Tolljur in his hands? Tolljur sought to bring the measure he had swallowed back up, to spit it into Friti's face, and succeeded in coughing out only a small portion. Horror gripped him even as, apparently satisfied, Gunnar strode away and Friti settled himself on the oak planking at Tolljur's side.

"You see, Tolljur," Friti said in a way almost conversational, "all is as it should be—or will be, soon, as it always should have been. We make bargains, we Vikings—it is how we live our lives, is it not? I made a bargain before I left home."

"With whom?" Tolljur tried to think, but his mind still did not seem to be working properly. Kaddi would never betray him. And Tiff was dead.

"Whom do you think? Come, you are a clever man, the sort who thinks he knows things—like whether or not I forced his sister."

Alarm speared through Tolljur, and his heart began to beat at an accelerated rate. Was that the poison taking hold? But he had not ingested much.

Perhaps it would not take much.

"Did you?" he gasped. If Friti at last admitted the truth, here beneath this jeweled sky, it meant Friti believed Tolljur would die.

"How dare she spurn me, the wretched girl—me, son of the jarl! How might she scorn my offer of marriage. *Ja*, did she tell you that part of it? Did Gyda not say how I honored her? She told me *nei*, and she spat at me, with disdain and hate in her beautiful eyes. I made up my mind then I would have her—no matter what she said."

Rage coursed through Tolljur's blood, not the familiar berserker rage but that of a man angered in defense of one he loved. He struggled to rise, but a strange lethargy added to the weight of his wounds and made it hard to so much as breathe.

Friti needed no encouragement to go on. "I have plucked many women, Tolljur Magnussen—many slaves and both my virgin wives—but I enjoyed Gyda most of all. She fought and struggled, but that only made it sweeter. I had her again and again—and I told her if she wished I would still take her for wife."

Tolljur's hands clasped frantically into fists.

"Everyone wondered why I had not married before then. I'd waited you see, waited for her. If the foolish wench had not killed herself…"

"You killed her." The accusation sounded hoarse and hung in the darkness between them. "With the harm you caused and the torment in her mind—you did."

"She had only to be sensible and accept me. I am a

prize. Why would she refuse?"

"You are the excrement of a troll."

"So you may say. But ask yourself, Tolljur Bearshirt, who will win now? You lie there powerless. And I have my bargain."

"With whom?" Tolljur asked again. "Who gave you the poison?"

"Women know things—what draughts to take, perhaps to be rid of unwanted babes, or enemies. One woman in Husavik you spurned too long."

"Anaborg."

"You—with your new wife—have become a problem, Tolljur Bearshirt. I shall rid us of you here and she shall rid us of your wife back home."

Eadha. Tolljur's pulse leaped so powerfully, blackness blotted out the stars.

He barely heard Friti above his own heartbeat, when the chief's son went on, "Then I—and my wife— will be first among our people. But rest now. You face battle in the morning—if you survive that long."

Chapter Thirty-Two

Eadha awoke from a troubled sleep and attempted to stir. Her limbs felt weighted, and her heart struggled in her breast, heaving in great, shuddering beats.

The room lay far too still. She could see the embers of the fire glowing in the central hearth and a motionless figure beside her that, when she blinked, resolved itself into Meghan, fast asleep.

She fought her way up from the bed, but the lass did not wake. On the pallet in the corner she saw Brida slept as well, and nearer the door Kaddi sat, also sleeping. Had the old man stayed to guard her? Yet he never stirred when Eadha got to her feet and tiptoed past him to the door.

Outside, the world lay in hushed patterns of black and silver, as if under enchantment. Eadha stood bemused, remembering the old tales spun by the elders back home, of spells cast and time suspended.

Overhead, the vast dome of the night glowed with stars. It must be very late, for the gloaming had faded, as much as it ever did at this time of year. To the northeast she fancied a rim of light showed above the water that reached to the horizon. Nothing moved, not even a breeze, and she felt utterly alone.

Perhaps she slept still. Aye, that must be it. Because after chasing magic so hard, so long, why would an enchantment that froze the world find her here and now, so far from home?

Tolljur. His name whispered in her mind, and fear tightened her chest. Where was he now? How was he? The berserker rage she'd sensed earlier must have fallen from him, but now—now another danger held him in its grip.

She did not know how she knew—she just did, as completely as if he'd conveyed it to her across the dark distance. She stood struggling to breathe through a sudden onset of horror, and all at once saw someone— something—moving on the slope below the hut.

Climbing. The one figure stirring in all this enchanted night.

Bemused, she stood and watched the figure make its way toward her, winding steadily between the huts below. It had come from the water then, from the shining sea. And it glowed with its own faint light.

A man he was, she saw when he drew near enough—not Tolljur. Too tall to be Tolljur, he was also too slim, and he moved with smooth grace. Silver like the moonlight, he had long pale hair that hung down his back, and he seemed to flicker in and out like the moonlight itself.

When he paused on the path in front of Eadha, she ceased to breathe at all. She knew him then by his beautiful face and his shining strength.

Lugh.

Often had she called upon him; sometimes she'd felt his presence. Never, never before had she beheld him. Now the world stopped and the stars froze in their paths through the sky as he looked into her eyes.

"Child," he said in her tongue—his own tongue— and the sound of his voice reverberated through her like the plucking of a magical harp string. She wanted to fall on her knees but could not move even for that.

If she died now, she knew she would be complete. But nay, nay—for a piece of her heart, the best and largest part, lay distant outside her breast.

"You think upon him who loves you," the god said, speaking not aloud so much as to her mind. "You must go to him. He needs you now."

"Go to him?" Eadha wondered.

"Even as you did before."

"But I was carried thence by the strength of the bond between us, born of the berserker's madness. All lies quiet this night. How might I reach him?"

"The bond between you still holds true. And look," Lugh said, and gestured behind.

A second figure came up the slope, the sole thing now moving in that patterned landscape. This one— female—trailed both hair and skirts, and Eadha's eyes narrowed. "Anaborg."

Lugh turned back to her. "She comes to take your life. You must accept the stroke. It is your means to go to your man. Have you courage enough?"

"Eh?" Eadha did not comprehend. She could now catch Anaborg's emotions, and her entire being cried out in warning. *Danger*. "Accept the stroke?"

"Trust me," Lugh bade.

Aye and how could she do otherwise? She'd sought all her life to follow this being, this single light. Could she find it in her to doubt him? Could she find the courage to obey?

Anaborg's emotions increased in intensity as she approached, unfurling like a wall of storm: hate and determination. In response, alarm threatened to close

Eadha's throat. Lugh reached out swiftly as if to touch her.

"Nay, child. Let it come."

What came was Anaborg's rush of surprise when she beheld Eadha standing in the doorway. She stumbled to a halt, and the rasping breath caught in her throat.

She hissed between her teeth, "Sisst! What are you doing out here?"

Did Anaborg not see the shining figure standing at Eadha's side? Nay, but Eadha caught the gleam of the weapon grasped in Anaborg's fist. Starlight raced along it when the woman raised it high.

"I am waiting for you," Eadha replied. "You've come to murder me in my bed. Did you not think you would be heard? Or seen?"

"I can move without sound when I wish—like a shadow." Anaborg sneered. "Anyway, here you are, making it easy for me."

Eadha stiffened. Lugh could not mean for her to stand and take what must be a death stroke? Had she strength enough, faith enough for that? Yet her god had spoken, and so it must be. She watched Anaborg's weapon rise still higher in an arc before it began to fall and, in that instant, felt Lugh's strength surround her in a wall of protection.

The blade bit flesh—bit once—before Eadha cried out, a call like a sea bird, that shattered the night's enchantment.

She crumpled and tumbled to the ground. But nay; that was just her flesh. Her spirit rose, buoyed by Lugh's strength.

"And now," he whispered in her mind, "you may

go to him."

She gathered herself and, precisely like a sea bird, flew up and over the water.

****

Morning broke, bleeding red on the eastern horizon. Tolljur pried open his eyelids and regarded the sight as the bad omen it could only be. Pushed by a wall of cloud, the starlit night fled on the breath of disaster.

The poison, he discovered with some surprise, had not killed him. Perhaps he had not swallowed enough of it after all. But it had destroyed what remained of his strength. He wondered bitterly whether that had been Friti's aim—he wanted to ruin Tolljur's vigor so he would perish in the battle to come.

At the moment, he could not imagine entering battle. Though his heart still pounded the blood through his veins in great, shuddering beats, he had not the strength to lift his hand, much less a weapon.

Around him he heard the crew begin to stir. Footsteps approached him where he lay tucked at the rear of the ship. Friti? But *nei*—instead he saw Mikka's face float into view above him and crease with alarm.

"Tolljur? Tolljur, you are unwell?"

"*Ja*—" The word stuck in Tolljur's throat.

Mikka hunkered down beside him. One hand came out to touch Tolljur's shoulder. "By Odin's eye, man, you are cold as death. You need a draught."

"No draughts," Tolljur grunted. He vowed another would never flow past his lips.

"I will fetch Jarl Gunnar."

Mikka hurried off, and Tolljur gathered all his might in an effort to move under his own power. *Ja*, Gunnar would come, and Friti with him. Tolljur must be on his feet then.

But how?

He lay watching the blood-red clouds race overhead, chasing the night.

Please, Odin.

Something moved next to him, close against his side. "Here, take my hand."

He turned his head and stared into Eadha's eyes. Ach, once more—by grace or by magic—she had come to him! So powerful was his gratitude, it lifted him.

Perhaps, after all, he lay dead. Friti's poison might have done its work and he had entered the afterlife. If so, he did not care. If death meant he might be with Eadha forever, he would gladly sacrifice Valhalla.

"You, here," he croaked. "Am I dead?"

"Not yet, and no' if I can prevent it." Her hazel eyes gleamed with a hint of silver in the garish morning light. "I ha' been allowed to return to you, summoned by your need. Here, my love, give me your hand."

He raised it somehow. She clasped it between both of hers and he felt her—real, substantial.

"So cold," she whispered. "You are far too cold."

Ignoring that, he told her, "They must not find you here. Friti—"

"They cannot see me." Her smile, wry and bleak, flashed at him. "Only you. Your god and mine have accomplished this thing."

"Together."

"Together, as we are together for always, Tolljur Magnussen. Now arise. We cannot let Friti see you like this."

"I have not the strength."

"Then take mine. All I have—all I am—is yours."

In that moment he knew it for truth. Yet for all her wit and intelligence—for all her magic—had she strength enough to replace his?

He could hear voices from across the deck of the ship. His fellow warriors came hurrying; Friti and his father would soon be here.

Help me, Odin, he thought.

Help me, Lugh, Eadha said at the same instant.

Then she merely slipped inside him, her spirit becoming one with his. Her strength flowed through his blood, warmed his flesh. It filled him as he sat, propped by his scarred and bloodied arms, and then, fighting the power of the poison, as he struggled to his feet.

He stood firm as a rock, with Eadha's will holding him, when Friti hurried up along with Gunnar and the other warriors behind them.

"By Thor's hammer," Friti exclaimed. "I expected you to be dead."

Chapter Thirty-Three

Tolljur stared at Friti with hard eyes. He could feel Eadha's anger filling him, holding him up, unflinching. It had little in common with his own berserker rage but seared hot as the smith's forge when flames temper the iron. At that instant Tolljur knew her to the root of his soul, better than he knew himself.

He turned his gaze on Gunnar. "Chief Gunnar, I cry foul. I have been betrayed."

Gunnar frowned and shook his head. "What is this?" he barked.

"Your son Friti expects to find me dead because he sought last night to assure it." Tolljur accused, "Friti Gunnarssen has fed me poison."

Gunnar shot a look at his son.

Friti took a rapid step backward, staring at Tolljur even as the men around them muttered. Swiftly he said, "*Nei*, not so. I speak as I do only because Mikka came running and told me the berserker was dead."

"I said no such thing." Mikka stepped up staunchly to Tolljur's side. "I said only that I found the berserker laid down."

Gunnar rounded on Friti. "What is the meaning of this?"

"Nothing—a mistake. Why would I harm the man we always follow into battle?"

"Why indeed?" Tolljur returned. Or was that Eadha

speaking through him? "Find the cup he gave me when I lay sore injured last night. Smell the potion. It is nothing Kaddi ever mixed for me. With Tiff dead, he saw his chance to be rid of me so he might be foremost of your warriors, Jarl Gunnar—and he took that chance. Find the cup, and ask Friti Gunnarssen to drink the dregs."

Friti backed another step, but others of Gunnar's warriors stood behind him; he could retreat only so far.

"Find the cup," Gunnar ordered bitterly, and Friti's gaze flew to him.

"Father—will you take the word of the berserker over me?"

Gunnar's expression hardened. "Tolljur Magnussen has never lied to me. I regret to say I cannot claim the same of you."

"In this, I have not lied."

Gunnar tossed his head. "From the time you reached my knee you lied. As soon as you could talk, you twisted the truth."

"Those were but fibs. Nothing like that of which the berserker now accuses me."

"Then, my son, look into my eyes and tell me the truth, if ever you have spoken it: is this thing true? Did you seek to poison Tolljur Magnussen?"

Friti's nostrils flared. "I already stand at the head of your warriors—those of us who fight under their own merit, that is. What reason would I have to destroy our best battle weapon?"

Tolljur announced before Gunnar could reply, "He already admitted to me he had forced my sister, Gyda, when she would not accept him. He acts out of spite and a long hatred."

"Speak!" Gunnar demanded of his son. "Is this true?"

Friti and his father stared long at one another. Friti uttered no word, yet his face spoke for him.

Gunnar's lips curled in disgust. "One thing you forget, Friti—I may tolerate you lying to others, but not to me, your father and your jarl. I have given you much leeway—far too much—in the hope you would become a man worthy of my place after me. But this act is without honor. You are without honor. I cast you off."

"*Nei*, Father, *nei*." Friti leaped forward and seized his father's arm. "This is but a tale woven by the berserker. If I did poison him as he claims, why is he not dead?" Friti shot a look at Tolljur where he stood, one full of superstitious horror. "It is magic. That wife of his—she has done this. She is accursed."

Tolljur raised his arm and delivered a blow across Friti's face, half punishment and half challenge. "Do not ever speak of my wife again. And if you would prove your innocence, face me in combat—here, now, on the deck of this boat. To the death. The gods will smile on whichever of us is in the right."

The men stared. Friti raked Tolljur with a glance through eyes gone suddenly wide.

There Tolljur stood—covered with wounds and barely able to keep his feet, yet Friti dared not move against him. Was it cowardice or fear of the gods' retribution?

The moment stretched long—far too long for Friti to recover from it.

At last Gunnar pronounced his judgment. "Guilty. Seize him, and may the gods wreak their justice upon him. Set the sails and draw anchor—we set our course for home."

Hear that, wife. Tolljur spoke to the woman inside him, only to find her gone. Her strength went with her, and he sank slowly down to the oaken deck.

I come to you, Eadha, he called after her. *I come home.*

****

From the place where he stood near the great, carved mast of the dragon ship, Tolljur could see people running toward the harbor as the ship sailed into Husavik's bay. Boys, men, women—no doubt some of them slaves—hurried like bees scenting honey, for word spread swiftly when a viking party returned home.

His heart quickened, not in the ragged beats prompted by Friti's poison but strong and deep, and he searched for one face among the many.

She must know he was coming. He had spoken to her nonstop in his mind since she left him, and all the while his sickness slowly abated. Though she'd not replied, he had been able to feel her presence.

But *nei*, Eadha's form did not appear among the many, though he saw Inger, as well as the girl Meghan from his hut. And, by the time the ship anchored and the skiffs were brought out, he saw Kaddi waiting also.

The old man stood full in the bright sun, looking far too ordinary, devoid of his raven-feather cloak, and far too grave for someone welcoming home a friend. Disquiet stirred in Tolljur's heart as he prepared to disembark, eyes still busy searching the shore, the whole time the skiff rowed in.

Kaddi and Inger met him together. The old man's hand came up to touch Tolljur's shoulder. "Praise Odin you have come. I have done all my skill allows." Kaddi gestured to Inger. "We both have."

"Eadha," Tolljur cried, and the men all around him stared. "What has happened?"

"Three nights ago she fell, attacked outside your door, by whom no one knows."

Tolljur's heart fell even as his jaw hardened. "I know who is responsible for this." He glanced behind him and found Gunnar. Time enough later to lay accusations. "Only take me to her," he bade his friends.

****

"She will not wake." The girl from the bath house, Brida, stood beside the bed and wrung her hands; Tolljur hunkered down, his own wounds forgotten.

The woman lying so still and cold in the bed could not be his Eadha—she looked like a carved image instead, waxen pale. Where was the life that always spilled from her, the energy and emotion? Where the fire that burned in her eyes?

They now lay closed like those of a corpse; her lips, slightly parted, showed no sign of breath.

He put one battered hand there and felt but the merest stir of air. *Ja*, she lived, but rested some place far distant from him.

"The knife stroke took her in the shoulder," Inger told him softly. "We do not think it struck the heart."

Nei, Tolljur thought, for Eadha had left her heart in his keeping.

Inger went on, "A bit lower and she would not be alive. Her girl heard something, arose, and found her almost at once." She nodded at Brida. "If not for that, she would have bled to death."

Tolljur looked at the slave. He corrected himself— former slave—who stood grave and silent. *Ja*, so

Eadha's kindness had been returned threefold, as the god promised.

In the girl's own tongue, he asked, "You saw no one?"

She shook her head. "Nay, but after I found my mistress, I thought little to look elsewhere."

"No matter," Tolljur stated. "I know the identity of her attacker." Friti had made no secret of it. And it would not take much now to make Friti confess all; his father's disapproval seemed to have demoralized him and removed most of his arrogant defiance.

All that could be settled later. For now, his attention must rest on Eadha and her survival. For upon her existence rested his own.

Chapter Thirty-Four

"Recall her to you," Kaddi bade Tolljur, not for the first time. "Speak to her so she may hear your voice."

"I have tried." Despair gripped Tolljur's heart. A day and a night since his return had he sat at Eadha's side. He had spoken to her, caressed her fingers, pleaded and demanded. She remained far from him, distant even in spirit.

Now night fell once more, the hazy gloaming through which stars peered down at him with cold eyes. Tolljur bowed his head over his hands, still clasped on Eadha's, and wondered how he could keep breathing if she slipped away from him.

Almost incomprehensible, how his world had changed since she entered it, how he had changed from a man made of stone to one whose heart bled. Easier, no doubt, to feel nothing, yet he would not trade the days and nights they had shared to save his own life.

To save hers, he would. At this moment he would trade anything including his freedom, his health, and his sanity.

At least her wound had stopped bleeding and had closed, a ragged hole that marred her left breast. Yet her strength did not return.

He knew why; she had spent all her strength on him, back on the dragon boat when she came so miraculously—so magically—in answer to his need.

Without thought for herself, she had given all she was for him, and he did not know how to return the favor.

Now, at the edge of the night, he, she, and Kaddi were alone, both girls gone elsewhere to snatch some rest. All had become quiet, so much that Tolljur could hear the soft breaths that barely lifted his wife's chest. Her only sign of life.

"She weakens," Kaddi pronounced with regret. "Boy, have you told her you love her? If not, do so now."

With that, the old man arose and left the dwelling. Pain welled up and flooded Tolljur's spirit, sharper than any ever taken in battle.

What good would it do now to offer Eadha his love? No prize, the love of a berserker, a man whose only purpose was to rage and fight. *Ja,* she represented the one light in his darkness. And if she winked out this night, like the stars at daybreak, he would abandon all hope.

"Eadha, wife," he whispered, "list to me. I love you. Do you hear?"

No sign, no reaction. Emotion blocked Tolljur's throat, and he could speak no more.

When had he last wept? At his father's death? At losing his mother, at losing Gyda? Since then he'd allowed little emotion to touch his heart, only anger. But Eadha had tapped something deeper in him, and now sobs came—ugly, gasping sounds that tore from his very spirit. There, alone, he wept his terror, grief, and need.

Do not leave me, he beseeched her in his mind.

And felt someone place a hand upon his shoulder.

Startled, he looked up expecting to find that Kaddi

had returned, unheard. But the being who stood beside him, though aged and indeed one-eyed, was not Kaddi.

He wore a dusty black cloak, and his white hair flowed down over it, as did his great beard. His single eye glowed like blue ice.

What will you be for her, my son?

Tolljur stared in disbelief even as a prick of enchantment traveled up his spine. He'd followed this god all his life without real hope of any meeting. Now, wholly caught in the magic of the moment, he sought to contemplate the question asked: not what will you bargain, not what will you give. *What will you be?*

He came to his feet as if hauled up by ropes, faced the old man, and whispered, "Father Odin."

The old man smiled, and the smile had the echo of far places in it, the roar of waterfalls in the fjords back home, the scream of eagles. It contained ineffable wisdom and knowledge. The single, ice-blue eye watched Tolljur with careful attention.

"Answer my question, son."

The breath stopped in Tolljur's lungs. If he spoke wrong now, he knew Eadha would slip away from him. And he did not know what answer the god sought.

"Not the berserker. I will not be that to her." He forced the words past his terror and knew their veracity when the old man nodded.

What more could he be? What else had he ever been? From a child he'd seen his father fall victim to the power of the rage and beheld his own destiny. What was he besides channeled madness and pain?

The answer came to him softly, like a whisper, like the vibration from one of Eadha's harp strings. To her, to Eadha, he was love.

He raised his head, and truth spoke through him. "I will be the man, the husband, she needs me to be."

The smile this time engulfed Odin's face, creased his wide brow, and wreathed his cheeks in joy.

"Dare you undertake the task of pleasing such a woman?"

"I dare, Father."

"It takes courage indeed, the kind perhaps found only in the heart of a berserker."

"Berserker no more," Tolljur vowed. "I renounce it and my past suffering, for her sake."

"Ah, my son, you have learned a truth of great value: love and anger cannot exist in the same heart. Is it worth the time you have spent on the tree of pain?"

Tolljur drew a harsh breath. "*Ja*, Father. It is worth the pain."

"Then pick up the harp."

"I do not play it, she does."

"And its music has, in the past recalled you from far places. Take it up."

Tolljur reached for the shadowy object that stood against the wall. It felt small and fragile in his hands. Yet he sensed a vibration flowing through it. Magic?

"Strike three notes," Odin instructed. *Three.*

Tolljur closed his eyes and let the magic take him. One note.

It trembled through the quiet night when he plucked a string with his great, clumsy fingers. Those fingers that had stroked Eadha's hair with a gentleness he'd never before employed.

A second, random string. He had smoothed these fingers, alive with desire, over his wife's breast.

The third note trembled and, with it, Tolljur's

heart. He remembered again the first time he had seen her in Gunnar's hall. The same impulse that had moved him then ruled him now. He had surrendered to something far more powerful than the rage.

Eadha. He called her as the last string sounded, across the distance.

****

A light appeared in the quiet darkness where Eadha floated. Purest silver and clearer than moonlight, it took an instant for her to tell it came from the being who appeared beside her...Lugh.

Outlined in silver he was, all grace and motion as he played upon a harp that appeared to be made of water—nay, silver foam. The tune was one Eadha had never heard, yet she knew it. Her spirit recognized the music of the waves upon the shore back home, the cry of seabirds, and Tolljur's rare laughter.

Tolljur.

Her heart ached for him as memory trickled back into her mind. Had she upheld him? Had he survived that terrible scene on the longship?

The tune Lugh played wound through her senses, reached her mind and then her heart. It carried her the way a wind carries the hint of far places, transporting her.

And all at once ceased.

List, the god said.

He plucked one note. Plaintively did it tremble, a question asked.

Aye, she replied.

A second note, and warmth came stealing through Eadha's limbs as it claimed her. She opened her eyes wider and breathed deep, feeling Tolljur's strength come flowing into her.

A third note, bright and victorious, and she felt her heart reply, an answer given.

Beside her, the god laughed in joy.

Chapter Thirty-Five

"I come to tell you I will serve as your berserker no longer." Tolljur's voice reverberated in the quiet morning. Eadha, on her feet beside him, felt his resolve, unflinching as ever his endurance in battle had been. Her fingers tightened on his, which twitched in response.

They'd gone to face Gunnar together, hands and spirits linked, as soon as Eadha mustered the strength to be out of her bed. In this thing they shared one mind.

Now Gunnar received them in his hall, empty at this time of day but for the slaves who tidied the place. These he dismissed with a grunt before he subsided into his great chair, looking unhappy.

"Tolljur Magnussen," he said, "this is not what I need to hear from you. You have been wronged, *ja*, and your sister before you." Out of courtesy, perhaps, he spoke in Eadha's tongue. "But surely we can make amends. Your service is far too valuable for me to lose. Whom else will you serve?"

"As berserker? No one. I renounce the practice." Tolljur glanced at Eadha, and she felt his love, steady and strong. "My wife and I—our whole house—will go to make a new life. I mean to buy from you what Alban slaves I can. I hope you will not deny me."

Gunnar looked surprised, and far from happy. After contemplating it, he said, "I will deny you nothing. But

I ask you first, before you take such a dire step as to leave Husavik, allow me to make amends."

Eadha turned her gaze on her husband. His ties here, she knew, ran deep. Would he reconsider this decision they had made together? But he shook his head.

"I cannot imagine, Jarl Gunnar, what you might offer me that would change my mind."

Gunnar leaned forward in his chair. "I will offer you recompense—anything you ask. Let us bargain together."

This time Tolljur's whole body twitched, an involuntary reaction.

He lifted his chin. "What recompense can you give for my sister's life? Has your son yet confessed his part in her death?"

Regret and acknowledgement mingled in Gunnar's eyes. "He has, and in so doing brings dishonor on my house. Your father, Tolljur, served me long and well. I held him in high esteem. For my son to harm his daughter sickens me. But you understand he did not kill her: she chose the act of taking her own life."

"He pushed her to that deed."

"And shall be punished for it."

"How?"

Gunnar hesitated only a moment. "What will satisfy you, Tolljur Magnussen?"

This too Eadha and Tolljur had discussed long into the night.

"Nothing can bring my sister back into this world. But I would be glad to know Friti Gunnarssen can no longer own the lives and freedom of other women, so to abuse them."

The Berserker's Bride

Gunnar looked at Eadha. "This sounds like your wife's desire rather than yours."

"Her desire is my desire," Tolljur said simply. "We have more to speak of, Jarl Gunnar, than your son's treachery. What of Anaborg Helmsdottir, who tried to kill my wife?"

"She is being held until I pass sentence upon her. You should know, Friti has stepped forward and offered to take her as wife, and so be responsible for her."

Tolljur laughed unexpectedly, a bitter sound. "Would you give one monster charge of another, Jarl Gunnar?"

"What choice have I? List to me, Tolljur Magnussen—I will banish them both if you agree to stay and serve me."

"And unleash them on the world?" Again Tolljur shook his head. "As I say, it is I, my wife, and our household who will leave."

"I will offer you a greater share of whatever we obtain in raiding—and higher status, if you remain at Husavik."

"Jarl Gunnar, I have all the wealth I require, enough to purchase a ship and procure what I need to sail." With absolute finality, Tolljur said, "You can offer me nothing beyond what I have asked."

Gunnar bowed his head in acceptance. "Where will you go?"

Tolljur's fingers tightened on Eadha's once more. "You may recall, Chief, those fair islands past which we sail on the way to raid in Alba—set amid the sea and barely occupied. My wife and I think to settle there—in the Faroes—and build a settlement neither Norse nor Alban, one founded in peace."

"Peace? A berserker?" Gunnar's lip curled. "You mean to sacrifice all you are—for her?"

"Come, wife," Tolljur said quietly. "We have wasted enough time here."

"You shall regret this!" Gunnar called after as they walked from the hall. "The Faroes, as well as anywhere else in this world, can be raided. You had better build your new settlement strong."

Chapter Thirty-Six

"And husband, have you any regrets?" Eadha inquired of Tolljur, as they sailed from the bay at Husavik a fortnight later with all their worldly possessions and a large number of former Alban slaves on board. They sailed southeast toward home, but Eadha knew she would never go to Harris again. Rather, this man at her side had become her true home.

Did he feel the same? He'd grown up in this green land of ice and steam.

"Regrets?" Tolljur echoed, musing. "Perhaps only that I did not slay Friti where he stood, in return for what he did to my sister."

They'd gone together to see both Friti and Anaborg before they embarked. Friti appeared a broken man, the loss of his father's esteem and favor reducing him to a shadow of the arrogant bully he had been. Anaborg—clearly now a madwoman—had spat and raved at them, worse than any berserker.

Eadha turned and looked at her husband. As usual he appeared stoical, but she knew better now, had tasted the emotions that lay beneath that calm like a current beneath a quiet ocean: strength and courage, compassion beyond measure. And love.

She drew a deep breath. "I was proud of you today, husband."

He turned his clear-water gaze on her in surprise.

"*Ja*? Why?"

"You did not let spite or anger overtake you, even though you had just cause. You did not fall victim to your rage."

"No more playing the part of the berserker," he vowed. A rare smile curved his lips. "Playing the part of your husband will require courage enough."

"You had best believe it. And no more of Kaddi's vile potions."

"*Nei*."

The old man had decided at the last moment to come with them, electing to start a new life despite his advanced age. Eadha felt a quickening at the idea of studying with him and perhaps sharing some of her own knowledge and beliefs.

She did not know for certain what their new life would bring, but it would be colored by love, faith and music. Tolljur had wrapped her harp with his own hands and stored it aboard his ship most carefully just before they sailed.

"I cannot live," he'd told her, "without the sound of your music in my ears."

Whatever befell them, they would not be lonely, Eadha thought now, stealing a look over her shoulder at their company. A score of former slaves—newly freed—accompanied them and most surprisingly almost as many Norse warriors, most of them young and all of them fellows who had followed Tolljur into battle. Mikka had come at their head.

"We have talked it over, Tolljur Magnussen, and would continue to follow you into this new beginning you describe."

Tolljur, perhaps remembering Gunnar's implied

threat, gratefully accepted the gift of fealty. He would lead this group—not as Gunnar had, but with measured strength and justice.

Eadha, never one to hold her tongue, would assure it. She felt great hope for their future, her one grief lying in the fact that no price Tolljur offered could persuade Harald to release Catrin. She and Eadha had clung together at parting, vowing to remain always friends.

The water between their ship and Husavik widened even as the future beckoned them. Eadha, examining her heart, found but a single longing more.

With a small smile she leaned up and whispered in her husband's ear, "Since you ha' renounced the place of berserker, husband, might I ask for a boon?"

Standing with his arms crossed on his chest, he gave her a look that combined love, stern tolerance, and humor. "What more, wife? Have I not already given you all I have?"

"Not quite."

"*Ja*, but I have: all my wealth, all my possessions. My life." His voice softened. "My love."

"One thing more." She flicked his ear with her tongue and felt a shiver of desire travel through him. "I want your bairns. Daughters, sons, all strong, brave, and true."

"Eadha, *nei*…"

Suddenly serious, she interrupted, "I know how you feel about this, Tolljur. But I ask you to think again. If born, our children will no' be raised in Husavik. They will never see a berserker rage. If you can learn to conquer that madness, so can any son I bear. I ask you, husband: place your faith in this future we go to build together, one founded not on battle and strife but peace and love."

"Ah, Eadha, but we may still be required to defend our shores, and this settlement we go to build."

"If it comes to that, I will stand and fight at your side. For never again shall you be sent to stand alone."

He caught her face between his hands; pure devotion looked at her from his eyes.

"From the first moment I saw you, wife, I have been able to deny you nothing. Even were I still berserker, I would not have courage to begin now."

"Then kiss your bride, Tolljur Magnussen."

With no further encouragement, he did.

A word about the author...

Award-winning author Laura Strickland delights in time traveling to the past and searching out settings for her books, be they Historical Romance, Steampunk, or something in between.

Born and raised in Western New York, she's pursued lifelong interests in lore, legend, magic, and music, all reflected in her writing.

Although she enjoys travel, she's usually happiest at home not far from Lake Ontario, with her husband and her "fur" child, a rescue dog.

Thank you for purchasing
this publication of The Wild Rose Press, Inc.

For questions or more information
contact us at
info@thewildrosepress.com.

The Wild Rose Press, Inc.
www.thewildrosepress.com

To visit with authors of
The Wild Rose Press, Inc.
join our yahoo loop at
http://groups.yahoo.com/group/thewildrosepress/

www.ingramcontent.com/pod-product-compliance
Lightning Source LLC
Chambersburg PA
CBHW051537260626
47170CB00003B/972

* 9 7 8 1 5 0 9 2 2 8 4 7 8 *